Grace Restored Series, Book 2:

Winter's Verdict

C.J. Peterson

Texas Sisters Press, LLC

C.J. Peterson

ISBN 978-1-952041-05-1

Published by Texas Sisters Press, LLC. Lufkin, TX U.S.A.

Texas Sisters Press, LLC.
2020

Second Edition

This book is dedicated to my loving husband and dear family who love and support me. You all mean more to me than you will ever know. Thank you! I love you!

A portion of the proceeds will be donated to Hope's Door, whose mission is to offer intervention and prevention services to individuals and families affected by domestic violence and to provide education programs that enhance the community's capacity to respond. To learn more about them, check out their web page: http://www.hopesdoorinc.org/

To learn more about C.J. Peterson, you can find her online at: http://cjpetersonwrites.com/

'While the stories are fiction, the journey is real!'

<u>Summary</u>

Winter's Verdict is the second book in the *Grace Restored Series*. After graduation from high school in the small Oklahoma town of West Springs, Katie MacKenna decided to start her life over in Cleveland, Ohio. Taking into account her roommate and closest friend over the last couple of years in college, Jillian Shaw, was murdered by a serial rapist on campus just before break, Katie chose to stay on the nearly deserted campus instead of returning home to her abusive father. During break, she is approached with an opportunity that may affect her aspirations to be an FBI agent. In the meantime, she also builds a friendship with Giovanni, the mafia leader's son. Things around her are confusing at best. Can she trust what is right before her when everything is not as it seems? Will her heart experience a winter thaw or will she forever be known as the Ice Queen?

John 3:19-21

[19] This is the verdict: Light has come into the world, but people loved darkness instead of light because their deeds were evil. [20] Everyone who does evil hates the light, and will not come into the light for fear that their deeds will be exposed. [21] But whoever lives by the truth comes into the light, so that it may be seen plainly that what they have done has been done in the sight of God.

Table of Contents

<u>Preface:</u>

Scenes from Book 1 of the Grace Restored Series

SEASONS OF CHANGE

Jill met Katie halfway across the quad. The snow was about a foot deep, and was continuing to float down in large flakes, slowly covering the footprints the students made in the fields. "Want to go to the library?"

"You want to go to the library on a Friday night?" Katie asked, stunned. "Isn't Cierra's party tonight?"

"Yep. I also know you have a paper due tonight. I'm hoping you will get it written in the library and can speed type like you do, to turn it in before we leave for the party."

"He said I could email it," Katie said, thinking about the possibility.

"C'mon! You aren't going to be able to be with me for Christmas. The least you can do is come to the party."

"Is Aaron taking you?"

"He is."

"I don't want to be a third wheel."

"You know, I could have someone join us so you won't feel that way," she hinted.

Katie narrowed her eyes. "Oh! I knew there was a method to your madness."

Jill burst out in laughter.

Katie huffed at her reaction. "Who is it?"

"Ethan?" she said, with hope in her voice. "Or if you want, I can have Seb in a heartbeat."

"Seriously? They're both great looking guys. I don't understand why they don't date?"

"Because both are enamored with you. Face it, you're a hot tamale. Ethan has admired you since day one, and Seb fell for you at first sight. They're both good guys. There aren't many of those left."

"I don't want to rush."

"I have *never* heard of two and half years *ever* being called a 'rush,'" she pointed out, as they walked to the library.

"I just don't want to see either one hurt."

"You're hurting them by not choosing."

"I'm hoping they will find other interests," she admitted.

"Tell ya what," Jill proposed, "What if Ethan rides over with us and Seb meets us there after work? I promise you they will just be happy you're there. Everyone was upset when Cierra told them you weren't coming."

Katie opened the door to the library. She paused, turned to Jill, and said, "Let me think about it."

"I'll take it!" She squealed in excitement. The joy that lit her face made Katie feel guilty for having to possibly tell her 'no' later. "You won't regret it. So, you think about an hour or so in here, and then type it out and email it in? Maybe leaving the dorm by seven?"

"I'll think about it," Katie reluctantly agreed, knowing she would have to agree or break Jill's heart…along with each one of her friends.

*   *   *

Katie went in search of a couple of books about Benjamin Franklin deep in the shelves of the library. She was over in the section searching, when a guy approached her. He was six foot two, had jet-black hair, and these deep, dark chocolate brown eyes. Katie couldn't take her eyes off of his while he almost seemed to float over to her. "Hi," he said.

"Hi," Katie nervously greeted him, tucking a portion of her hair behind her ear.

He shook her hand as he introduced himself, "I'm Giovanni Rossi."

"Katie MacKenna. Italian?"

"Very much so. Is it that obvious?" He smiled a shy smile.

"Afraid so."

"Irish?" he asked her.

"Is it that obvious?"

"Sort of. The pale skin, freckles on your nose, and green flecks in your eyes were a pretty good clue, but the pendant on your necklace left no room for doubt," he said, picking up the Celtic cross she always wore around her neck.

"Uh, yeah." Her face flushed bright red as she took the necklace her mother gave her as a young child back from his grasp.

"Anyway," he leaned on the stack of books, "I was hoping you could help me."

She narrowed her eyes. "With what?"

"Well, I've seen you here before, so I know you know your way around here. I am having some trouble looking for a book on Thomas Jefferson. I have this paper due in American History by tonight. I have a good portion of it written, but there are still —"

"Professor Miller?" she asked, cutting him off.

"Yeah. How did you know?"

"We're, um, in the same class. Mine's on Ben Franklin," she said, holding up her book.

"Ohhh, so I'm not the only one sneaking in at the eleventh hour," he said in relief.

It was endearing to her that he seemed so vulnerable, so honest. "No, you're not."

"Um, okay, I will admit this to you, and no one else, but I have no idea how to work this computer system thingy. I have tried, but I usually end up bribing someone to help me find what I need," he admitted.

"So, you don't know how to use it at all?"

"No."

"Well, I'll tell you what…so you don't have to bribe anyone else again, I'll show you how it works. And, your secret will be safe with me."

"Agreed," he said, shaking her hand. "Katie MacKenna, if you can help me figure this out, you will be my hero."

* * *

With a sense of urgency written all over her, Jill yanked Katie down the aisle away from Giovanni. When she was certain he was out of earshot, Jill hissed, "I can't take you anywhere!"

"What's your problem?" Katie asked, wriggling her way free from Jill's grip.

"Don't you know who that is?"

"Sure. He said his name was Giovanni Rossi. What's the problem?"

"He's from the Rossi family," she exclaimed.

"Well, duh! That's why his last name is Rossi. Nothing gets by you."

"Shhhhh!" Mrs. Marshall hissed from across the library.

"I swear that woman has hawk ears," Jill sighed. She lowered her voice, as she explained, "Yes, he's from the Rossi family, as in a *family* family."

"What are you talking about?" Katie whispered. Jill gave her a look. At first Katie was confused, until the thought registered in her mind. "Are you serious? Are you talking mafia family?"

Jill nodded. "They are *very* well known around here. I'm surprised you haven't heard of them."

"No. I haven't. So, are you saying everyone avoids him because of what his family does?"

"There are actually two of them. His little brother, Joey, is a freshman here too."

*   *   *

"You are being disrespectful by continuously cutting her off. Are you going to cut that out?" Giovanni glared at Ethan as he, Ethan, and Katie stood by the mailroom that night, where Katie and Giovanni had just mailed their papers to their professor.

Ignoring Giovanni, Ethan asked, "Are you ready to go back?"

"Yes. Thank you, Giovanni, for standing up for me, but Ethan's fine," Katie explained.

"Are you sure?"

"Yes. I appreciate you making sure, but he's a good guy. Ethan, would you mind walking me back to the dorm?"

"Of course."

"Thank you for your help earlier," Giovanni exclaimed. "Have a good weekend and I'll see you on Monday."

"See you on Monday," Katie said before they left the mailroom.

When they were outside and cleared of the building, Ethan asked, "Are you feeling better now?"

Katie looped her arm through his as she admitted, "I was afraid to come on my own, but I thought you guys were at the party already. I know Seb called when he was off work, but I wasn't ready yet."

"I know. He called me. I picked up a couple extra hours on security so I could be available later. I was wandering around campus, keeping an eye on things while I waited for you to call. If you didn't call in an hour or so, I would have stopped by the dorm."

Katie stopped and knelt down, picking up something out of the snow.

"What is that?" Ethan crouched down next to her.

"It's a shoe. Kind of weird, but it looks like the one Jill bought last week when we went to the store."

"You were in a store around Christmas?"

"We were looking for shoes for her Christmas outfit. This is her and Aaron's fifth year anniversary."

"I see. Are you sure it's hers?" He studied the shoe, noting it was partially covered in snow.

"Pretty sure. It's the same size, too."

Ethan glanced around the immediate area. Feeling the hair on the back of his neck rise, he pulled her up with him. Keeping his arm around her, he ushered her toward the dorm in the most direct route.

They were about a hundred yards from the dorm, when Ethan stopped and turned Katie into him. "What are you doing?" she demanded, shoving him away. Seeing him staring in horror toward the bushes running along the dorm next to theirs, she turned to see what he was looking at.

She gasped, covering her mouth. "Is that…?" her voice trailed off.

"Go to the dorm and call 9-1-1," Ethan ordered.

"No, I…no," she said, and ran over to the bushes before he could grab her. What she ran up to would be forever cemented in her mind. She knelt on the snow next to the body of her best friend. Brushing Jill's hair aside exposed all of the blood and red marks visible on her throat and face.

*   *   *

Stacey stayed the entire night with Katie, and into the weekend. When Jill's family came to the dorm the following Monday to clear her room, Katie did her best to help them. Working in the daze she functioned in over the weekend, she was able to separate herself from what was going on around her.

The day exams were finished for the semester, she watched several students from within her dorm as they packed up their stuff to leave the school and not return. The attacks were bad enough, but the attacker had escalated to murder. Very few students felt safe and decided to take Christmas break to make a final decision on whether to complete their education at Cleveland State.

Katie stood her ground, though. She was not going to let someone push her away from her dream. She was only a year and a half from graduation. She treasured her friends. She did ask to change apartments, though. It broke her heart to walk into that room each day. Her group of friends, along with Stacey and Scott helped her move to a private room before the break began. Stacey begged Katie to come to her house for the break, but Katie knew she needed the time. If she were going to embrace God and His words, if she were going to trust Him, they needed to have some serious discussions. It would also take time for her to sort through her thoughts and feelings.

As the remaining students left who were going to leave the dorms for Christmas break, Katie went over to the window of her new room, which she had to herself. She pressed her hand on the ice-cold glass and cleared it, to see the snow falling to the ground in large flakes. Pushing open the window, she looked toward the Heavens. "All right. You want me to trust You? I'll make you a deal. You show me You're real this break, show me You care about me, that You love me, and I will trust You. I will put my full trust in You and I will walk with You for whatever life I have left. It's up to You. Show me."

Chapter 1

The Fleece

Seventeen-year-old Damian wandered around the warehouse district that had been his home since he ran away from his abusive uncle at age thirteen. After his parents died in a car accident when he was five, his uncle took him in and never let him forget it.

Covered in filth, his jeans, sneakers, and jacket all had holes in them, but he did his best to change them out once in a while with the money he made from odd jobs. Additionally, he was granted the blessing of being a snitch to FBI agent Nick Locke. When Damian had information for him, Nick would buy him lunch. He would also buy Damian clothing when his looked a little too worse for wear.

Damian didn't like living on the streets, but he would rather go looking through the restaurant dumpsters for his food, than take beatings or be belittled by his uncle each day. Deciding his best bet not to be found would be to hide in a city in another state, he ran from Erie, Pennsylvania to Cleveland, Ohio.

Nick stumbled onto him by happenstance. One night, when Damian was fourteen and searching for food in an alley, he witnessed a murder committed by Dante from the Rossi family. When Dante saw him, he slammed Damian into the wall. Thinking he'd killed him when Damian slid down the brick wall, unconscious, leaving a blood trail, he left Damian for dead.

When the officer responded to an anonymous call regarding the murder, he found Damian still there. Through the course of the investigation, the detective assigned the case discovered the murder victim was a witness to another crime committed by the Rossi family. He immediately contacted the agent in charge of the case, Nick Locke. Damian made the concession to talk to Nick, as long as he wasn't used in any formal paperwork or in the trial. As soon as Damian described the assailant, Nick instantly knew it was Dante. Since Nick needed the information Damian had, he respected Damian's request. From that day forward, Damian became another set of eyes and ears on the street for Nick.

Damian's coat was in shambles, but he did his best to tuck it around his body as an icy chill cut through the buildings, creating frigid wind tunnels. He normally didn't venture out during the day, but he needed food, and it was too cold at night to search. With temperatures hovering at about fifteen degrees and wind chill factors hanging around three degrees, any amount of warmth generated by the sun was welcome.

A scream echoed over the whistling wind and he stopped in his tracks. Flattening himself against the wall in the shade, he strained to listen over his now racing heartbeat. In the building across from him, he heard the screams again. He slowly crept toward the building to a window that had already been broken.

On his tippy-toes, he peeked through the tiny hole to see a woman zip-tied to a chair, next to a table that contained a car battery, jumper cables, and a set of torture tools. There were two men beating on the woman, while a third yelled in her face, shouting in a foreign language. Her left eye was swollen shut, blood covered her torn clothing, and there were cuts and bruises visibly evident all over her body. Damian wasn't sure how much more the woman could take and still be alive.

Dropping back down out of sight, he had to catch his breath. The horrific screams coming from the woman turned into shrieks when her captures hooked up a car battery with jumper cables and burnt her skin with the live charges.

His heart pounded so fiercely, he thought sure the men would hear it. Pulling Nick's card with his cell phone number from his pocket, Damian ran as fast as he could out of the warehouse area toward a gas station. Once safely there, he pulled the pay-by-use phone from his pocket that Nick had given him for such occasions.

"Agent Locke," Nick answered his phone.

"Nick, it's Damian."

"Hey, mate," Nick said, with his thick Australian accent, "been a while. Thought maybe ya lost your phone."

"Please just listen. I don't want to use too much of the time."

"No worries. I'll reload it next time we meet. What's going on?"

"There's a woman being tortured in the warehouse district."

"Did you recognize anyone?" Nick asked, with a sense of alarm in his voice.

"No, but the guys were talking funny."

"Funny, how? With an accent?"

"Yeah, and in a foreign language."

"Can you tell me something they said as an example?"

"The one who was asking the questions at one point said to one of the other guys, '*nyet, ni nada.*'"

"That's Russian for, '*no, there's no need*,'" Nick translated. "Can you describe the woman?"

"She's pretty beaten up. From what I could see, she looked older than you. She had medium-length brown hair. Her one eye was swollen shut, so I couldn't really tell the eye color."

"Where is she?"

Writing down the directions Damian gave him, Nick passed them to the agent in charge of his unit, Seth Simmons, to set up for a rescue. Before Nick hung up with him, he set up a time to meet with Damian to take him out to lunch. If his information was good, Nick was sure he would owe him more than a lunch. Last time he saw him, Damian's coat was looking ragged, so he planned to take him a new winter coat as well.

When he hung up, Nick took a moment to collect his thoughts. He had a sick feeling in his stomach that this might be Diane Foster, an agent from their unit who went missing the week before. He wasn't sure whether to pray his hunch was right or wrong. If he was right, he'd finally found her. However, by Damian's description, she was in rough shape. If he was wrong, she was still missing. Time was of the essence either way.

*   *   *

"Unit two, head in through the back while we take the front," Special Agent in Charge, Seth Simmons, said into his radio. Seth stood at six-foot-two, with dark-brown hair and brown eyes. Even with his thin build, his tactical gear made him look bulky. Truth be told, he was all muscle, but didn't look it, especially next to his partner, Nick Locke.

Nick was known as the brawn of the unit. At six-foot-four, his immense presence was felt as soon as he stepped into a room. His charisma and good looks of blond hair, sky-blue eyes, and pure muscle, were never missed. His Australian accent added to his charm, making him virtually impossible for women to resist. They often used him to get the attention of the women, and work his way into the situations they needed him to infiltrate.

"Ready and in position," the agent in charge of the other unit responded.

"On the count of three, we enter. Be advised, we know her location, so we'll retrieve Agent Foster," he said, making sure they didn't take out one of his squad. She had been undercover among the Rodchenko Crime Family for several weeks.

"Copy that," the other agent responded.

"One, two, three," Seth counted.

Shouting, yelling, and gunfire rang from every direction in the warehouse as the agents penetrated both entry points. They were greeted with a barrage of gunfire from the Rodchenko family members who currently occupied the building. This went on for several long, tense minutes while agents from several other units followed after them.

When the gun fire all but stopped, Agent Claire Brenner gave Seth instructions over a headset from the safety of a mobile unit just down the road. "Go to your left," she said, as she sat behind the computer screens, with Agent Emma Sharpe looking over her shoulder. Several screens showed the cameras on the helmets of the men in a split screen view, and a single one that contained blue prints of the warehouse itself.

"According to Nick's source, she should be in the room down that hallway to your left, two doors down."

"Copy that," Seth said, quietly, unsure if there were more men from the Rodchenko family in the warehouse waiting to jump them. He gestured for the other two agents in his squad, Dakota Wolfe and Todd Edwards, to check the other room, while Nick picked the padlock on the door where Diane was being held.

Nick could pick any lock known to man in a matter of seconds – which made a more stealthy entry. Unless there was a barrier on the door, there was no need to kick a door in with him around. Of course, if that was the case, due to his strength he was often used for that as well.

After the lock was picked, Seth pushed open the door to see his agent tied to a chair. He heard Claire gasp into the radio at the vision of her friend and coworker on the monitor. Her face was hardly recognizable, and she had cuts, scrapes, and bruises all over her body, while blood coated her clothing. It was the interior wounds of broken bones and internal bleeding that were the bigger concern for Seth.

"Stop," the man behind her shouted, as he held a gun to Diane's head.

Seth put up his hands, with the gun still in his right hand. "Look, we're FBI. Put the gun down. We only want the woman."

"Ostanovka, ili ya ub'yu yeye," the man responded.

Seth glanced toward Nick for a translation. "He said, '*Stop, or I'll kill her.*'"

"Tell him to put the gun down," Seth told Nick.

Nick translated, "Opusti pistolet."

"Nyet!" the man shouted.

"Vy dolzhny poka my budem schitat' do trekh, ili my budem strelyat'," Nick ordered. The man's eyes widened as Nick translated for the others in the room, "I told him that he had until we counted to three or we would shoot."

Seth took the cue and positioned his weapon, aiming at the man's head.

"Odin," Nick said, starting to count.

"Otpusti menya , ili ya ub'yu tvoyego agenta!" the man threatened.

"He said to let him go or he'll kill our agent," Nick said, raising his weapon. Dakota and Todd aimed as well. Standing firm, Nick continued to count, "Dva."

The man cocked the gun that was aimed at Diane's head.

Nick fired his weapon, landing the bullet square between the man's eyes. The man's body slammed into the wall behind him as his gun went off. The stray bullet from the man's gun hit the wall next to Dakota's head while the man's body dropped to the ground. "Tri," Nick said when the room went silent.

Seth ran to Diane. While he released her from her ties with a pocket knife, he asked, "Did you give them anything?"

"Wouldn't be here if I did," she mumbled, barely moving.

"Let's get you out of here." Seth helped her out of the chair, but she burst into sobs, so he held her instead.

"We're clear," Nick said into his radio.

"All is clear out here as well," the other agent in charge announced.

"Ambulance just pulled up," Claire said into the radio, wiping the tears from her eyes. Then she muted her mic and said to Emma, "I don't think she could have taken much more."

"No. Thank God they found her," Emma mentioned, as she stood and began to pace, a thousand thoughts running through her mind.

Claire shook her head. "God had nothing to do with it. Our guys found her and rescued her. She's a strong woman."

"Not as strong as you think. She made it out of this one, but she's forty-three. Do you really think they're going to let her go undercover again?"

"No. I'm pretty sure she's headed into here from this point forward," Claire confirmed. Claire looked toward the screen to see the men gingerly lift her out of the chair. Twenty-seven-year-old Nick put her arm over his shoulder, supporting the weight of her body to help her out of the warehouse to the waiting ambulance.

"Then we'll need a new unit member."

"You mean another female," Claire corrected. "I'm afraid she's going to be a desk jockey for the remainder of her career if she chooses to return. Director Shaw wasn't happy when he found out her cover was blown and she was MIA. If it wasn't for that street kid of Nick's who heard her screams and figured out what room she was in, we would never have known where she was."

"Thank the Lord for little ones with ears."

"Quit giving credit to that God of yours. There is such a thing as luck, ya know."

"I don't believe in luck. I believe in God."

*   *   *

About a week into her Christmas Break, Katie was in her room doing her devotions. Remembering her challenge to God, she was reminded of a story Eric shared in youth group. She turned to Joshua 6, scanned down to verses 36-40, and read: "'Then Gideon said to God, *"You said that you would help me save the Israelites. Give me proof. I will put a sheepskin on the threshing floor. If there is dew only on the sheepskin, while all the ground is dry, I will know that you will use me to save Israel, as you said."* And that is exactly what happened. Gideon got up early the next morning and squeezed the sheepskin. He was able to drain a bowl full of water from it. Then Gideon said to God, *"Don't be angry with me. Let me ask just one more thing. Let me test you one more time with the sheepskin. This time let the sheepskin be dry, while the ground around it gets wet with dew. That night God did that very thing. Just the sheepskin was dry, but the ground around it was wet with dew.*'"

She got off her bed and opened the window. The rush of cold wind smacked her in the face as she looked out over the almost deserted campus. She calculated maybe twenty to thirty other students left on the campus with her who hung around for work purposes instead of returning home. The doors to the dorms were locked since there was no one in the lobby and security was on a skeleton crew. Whenever anyone returned to the dorm, security would have to let them in until break was over.

The snow and ice had been building for several days, but each day she would knock it off in order to open her window. The cold, fresh air reminded her she was alive and this wasn't some bad dream. She didn't want to be alone, but she didn't want to be a bother either. Losing Jill a week and a half ago cut her deeply. She thought she was done losing people. It made her want to not get close to anyone again. The verses Stacey and Scott shared with her that night touched her, but her jagged heart was growing cold. Maybe she *would* be the Ice Queen for the rest of her life after all.

She sighed before she looked up at the sky toward Heaven. "All right," she said to God, "I have a lot of respect for You. I put the challenge out to You, but I haven't heard anything yet. Please let me know You exist. I'm putting a fleece out like Gideon did."

Psalm 9:10 ran through her mind, *'Those who know Your name trust in You, for You, LORD, have never forsaken those who seek You.'*

"I *am* seeking You. People keep telling me You don't hate me, and You supposedly love me. I told You before if You want me to trust You, You have to show me You're real this break. Show me You care about me and I will trust You. I will walk with You for whatever life I have left. It's up to You, though. Show me. This is my fleece. This is my challenge to You."

Silence filled her room. The only sound she heard was the ice crackling on the trees and an occasional tree branch breaking under the weight of the snow, falling to the ground with a thud.

"Silence. All I get is silence. Fine. You have three more weeks to prove to me You're real and You love me. After that, we're finished."

Katie froze when she heard a knock on the apartment door. She looked down to the entrance of the dorm, noting no footprints on the walkway. "Hmmm," she said, cautiously going to the door. Looking through the peephole, she saw two men. One was about six-four, the other around six-two. Both were handsome and in suits and ties. She opened the door. "Look, guys, I appreciate your passion for your religion, but you scared me. I'm fixin' to call security if you don't leave."

They looked at each other before bursting out in laughter.

"That's a new one," the taller of the two said, his Australian accent evident.

They both produced their badges and IDs, which stated they were FBI agents. The taller one's name was Nick Locke and the shorter one Seth Simmons. Handing their IDs back to them, she nervously asked, "Um, what can I do for you? I'm not aware of anything I did."

"May we come in?" Seth asked.

She gestured to the table off the tiny kitchen of the apartment suite. "There's a table over there where we can sit."

When they settled, Seth spoke first, "We first wanted to extend our condolences regarding Jillian Shaw. We understand you two were roommates for two and a half years."

"Yes, sir, but –"

"Director Shaw is our supervisor," Nick explained, cutting her off. "His family was deeply hurt by her loss. We also know how close you are to the Shaw family."

"I am, but –"

"We understand you met with Giovanni Rossi on the night she was killed," Seth interrupted her.

"That's true, but he didn't kill her," Katie said adamantly.

"How do you know?" Nick asked. "Isn't it true she made it very clear to you to stay away from him?"

"She did, but he was writing his paper when Jillian was, um…" Katie swallowed her words, not wanting to admit to Jillian's passing aloud, while nervously fiddling with a napkin on the table.

"How do you know this?"

"Because she was missing by the time I got back to the dorm, per the note her boyfriend, Aaron, left her. Also, I helped Giovanni find the books he needed for his paper that night in the library, so I know he was there at the time she was killed. And, according to the way she looked, she had been dead for over an hour when we found her."

"How do you know that?"

"Criminology is one of my majors," she explained. "The amount of snow that covered her told us by the rate it dropped that night that she was there for over an hour. Now, knowing the time she left and the time I returned to the dorm, she had to have disappeared within the hour between when she left the library and when I returned to the dorm to write my paper. Giovanni was still in the library and didn't leave prior to that."

Seth sat back in his seat and crossed his arms. "How do you know?"

"Because I noticed him."

"Noticed him *how*?" Nick pushed, as he intertwined his fingers on the table in front of him.

"Well, he's kind of hard to miss," Katie said, as she felt her face flush in embarrassment by her admittance.

"So, you think he's good looking?"

Katie's anger momentarily flashed at what he'd insinuated. "What does that have to do with anything?"

"We're here to ask for your help," Seth admitted.

Katie crossed her arms, glaring at them. "What kind of help?"

"We would like you to befriend Giovanni," Nick explained.

"Why would I do that? My friends have continuously told me *not* to be friends with him."

Nick glanced at Seth, and Seth nodded, so Nick asked, "Can we trust you?"

"Pretty sure you wouldn't be here if that were in question."

Seth and Nick both laughed. "You're quick," Nick commented. After they settled, he clarified, "Let me correct myself. We know we can trust you, but we need to ensure whether you help us or not, that what is said here is left between the three of us."

"Why are you being so cryptic?" Katie asked.

"Because we just dropped off an agent at the hospital this morning and don't want a repeat," Seth said. "You see, we know you're interested in working for the FBI and only have about a year and a half left of school."

"Right."

"Well, we're asking if you want to do a sort of internship in working with us."

"In other words, I don't get paid."

"Correct."

"How much danger would I be in?"

"Danger is relative," Nick jumped back into the conversation. "We're only asking you to be friends with the guy."

"According to my friends, that's dangerous."

Seth let out a frustrated breath of air. "Okay, here's the deal. Giovanni is sick and tired of being the son of Lucca Rossi. He is the oldest and will inherit the family business when he is of age, but I can guarantee he wants nothing to do with it. He and his dad have a love/hate relationship."

"He loves him, but hates what his father does," Nick clarified. "He doesn't want the business. He hates that what his dad does has cost him so much."

"Meaning?" Katie questioned.

"Meaning his mother was killed when he was thirteen. Meaning he hasn't had a close friend, except for the men who work for his father. Meaning he has never had a girlfriend or gone on a date."

"Meaning he has not had a life because of his father," she said in understanding. "And if he continues on the track he's on, he won't have one either."

"We can't get anyone undercover into that family," Seth went on. "They are too closed off and exclusive. Having said that, Giovanni approached you, you didn't approach him. This means it was an innocent occurrence. You are both in a couple of the same classes next semester, too, so it will still seem innocent."

"What does this have to do with Jillian's death?" Katie asked, confused.

"We needed to clear him and you did that," Nick assured her. "Look, we're only asking you to keep your eyes open and report back to us what you see and hear. In the meantime, he gets a friend."

"How can this be done so he doesn't get hurt?"

"If it's done right, we may be able to get him to flip on his father, shutting that family down."

Katie sat back in her seat, nervously nibbling on her finger nails.

"With it being break, there aren't many people here to stop you from being his friend. A friendship can be established and you can help him in the process."

"Can I think about it?"

"Of course. We only wanted to put the fleece out there to see what you thought," Nick said, then pulled his card from his wallet. "Please let me know what you come up with." He wrote his cell phone number on the back of the card and handed it to her. "This is of the utmost secrecy. Only contact me."

"Yes, sir." Katie walked them to the door and locked it after they left. She looked toward the ceiling and said aloud to the Lord, "Nice. I'm pretty sure I'm supposed to do this, especially with the words that Nick guy used. If I do, I am asking You to keep me safe. I want to be one hundred percent sure, not just pretty sure. If You could make it obvious that I'm supposed to do this, I would appreciate it. You seem to have a hand in quite a bit, and I don't want to mess up anything. Also, would you mind finding Jillian's killer? I will only admit to You that it scares me to death to be on campus practically by myself, knowing there is a killer out there. This is my second fleece I am putting out to You. Please don't let me down now."

Chapter 2

Frozen in Time

Katie walked to the café around four o'clock for dinner that night. She made a deal with Dominic and Riccardo that if she could use the phone at Cook's Café to call security before she left, she would still be there for dinner. She didn't want to walk there alone, but with a practically deserted campus, and her lack of experience driving on ice and snow, she didn't have much choice. She hoped the light of dusk would be enough to deter anyone watching her.

She pulled the door and felt the rush of warm air as the 50's music enveloped her, creating an inviting atmosphere. It took her eyes a few moments to adjust to the brightness of the interior.

"Hey, there, beautiful," Dom called to her through the kitchen window.

"Hey, Dom," she called back, and headed over to the corner booth she and her friends usually occupied when school was in session.

Sebastian came out of the kitchen only a few moments later. He dropped off food at the counter for the young man sitting there before he went over to Katie's booth. He sat opposite her and said, "Lemonade is fresh, per Dom's orders. He also said if you wanted to, I could walk you back to your dorm and wait for security with you."

"That would be great. Thanks!"

"It's not all that busy." He shrugged. "Besides, I don't like some of the calls I've been getting from our friends lately. They aren't happy you're here by yourself, but due to family issues they can't have you over."

"Not a problem. I get it," she said, glancing through the menu. "What's fresh today?"

"Just about anything. It's going to take a bit longer, because they haven't premade much due to the break, and being the day before Christmas Eve."

"I would imagine. Okay, how about an order of fried chicken, mashed potatoes and gravy, and a small side salad?"

"Sounds good. Be back in a bit," Seb said, and bolted for the kitchen.

A moment later, Katie saw a shadow on the table. She turned and saw Giovanni awkwardly standing there. "Hey," he said, shoving his hands in his pockets. "I'm eating over at the counter and wondered if you wanted company?"

She gestured to the other side of the booth. "Sure. Have a seat."

He got his food and sat down across from her. "My Dad's in a meeting and my brother is at the gym."

"I see. What about your mother?"

"She, uh, died when I was thirteen."

"I'm sorry. Mine passed when I was seven."

"Really?"

"Yes. She died of leukemia. Yours?"

"Not sure if I should tell you."

"Why not?"

"Because you may think poorly of me, and I'm enjoying my anonymity."

"What does that mean?"

He sighed. "Maybe this is a bad idea."

"Wait." She put her hand on his arm when he moved to get up from the booth. Feeling his pulse quicken at her touch, she asked, "What's a bad idea? Being friends? How is having a friend a bad idea?"

"Boy, I can't leave you alone for a minute, can I?" Seb asked, setting her lemonade down. Glancing at her hand placement, he looked at her with a questioning look. He shoved his way into the booth on her side and said, "Hey, buddy, Katie and I need to talk. Can we have a minute?"

"No." Katie shook her head. "I invited him to eat with me."

Both guys turned to her, stunned.

"I think it's rude of you to push your way in here and ask my friend to leave. Now," she set her hand on Seb's shoulder, "You're my friend too, and we can talk later, but for now I'm enjoying my meal with Giovanni."

"You…are you serious?" Seb's face slowly drained color. "We *really* need to talk."

"I'll be fine. We can talk on the way back to the dorm," she offered.

"I'll take you up on that," he said. Continuing his conversation to Katie, he hinted to Giovanni, "I'll just be over there if there's anything you need, Katie. And, yes, I will walk you back to your dorm."

"Understood," Giovanni acknowledged what Seb had told him. In a manner of speaking, he'd laid claim to Katie.

After he left the table, Katie apologized, "I'm sorry about that. My friends seem to think they can dictate who I have as a friend."

"Is he your boyfriend?"

"Nope."

"Cool," he said, snacking on one of his fries.

"So, your mom?"

He almost choked on his fry as he asked, "What about her?"

"What happened to her?"

Clearing his mouth, he asked, "You promise not to think badly of me?"

"About your mother's passing? You're not the one who did it, were you?"

"Me? No!" Horrified, he responded, "No way! I loved her."

"Then, what happened?" she pressed.

He sighed. "Mom and Dad were having dinner at a fancy restaurant on Christmas Eve to celebrate their anniversary. Afterward, while they waited for the valet, there was a drive-by shooting."

Katie gasped, covering her mouth. "Oh my! I'm so sorry!"

"It was from another family," he admitted.

"I don't understand," she lied.

He looked her right in the eyes as he quietly said, "My father is head of the Rossi family, as in the Rossi crime family. The shooters were from a rival family in the area, the Rodchenko family."

"That sounds Russian."

"It is. They want my father's territory."

"I see," Katie said, stirring her lemonade with the straw. "So, is that what you're going to do when you're old enough?"

"Not if I can help it."

"Really? Why not? All that power and prestige? Why would you give that up?"

"Because that's only half of it. To me, all that power and prestige comes at a hefty price. My brother wants it, and I say more power to him. I want nothing to do with it."

"What do you want to do?"

He smirked. "Do you really want to know?"

"That's why I asked."

"I want to own a ranch in the country somewhere and be a veterinarian."

"Um, pretty sure you're in the wrong school for that one."

"I am. My major is accounting."

Shaking her head confused, she admitted, "I'm afraid I don't understand."

He sighed again. "My dad is paying for school. He wants me to be an accountant, but I have always wanted to be a vet. I love animals and the country is really quiet. I'm tired of city life."

"But, you seem so gruff, so –"

"So, not your standard vet?"

"Exactly."

"Obviously my dreams don't matter to him."

"Shame. You seem like a good guy."

A grin spread across his face. "Really?"

"Yeah. You seem to have a bad deal when it comes to your family, though."

"He's the one in control."

"And if he wasn't?"

"I wouldn't be here. I would be at an agricultural school, with veterinary medicine as my major. Some of my electives are science based, though he hasn't figured that out yet. I did that in case I could sneak that major in at a later date."

"I see."

Seb brought Katie's food to the table. "Dom added an extra serving of potatoes and gravy because he said it looks really cold out there and you need more meat on your bones."

"Tell him 'thank you,'" Katie said with a chuckle.

After he left, Giovanni asked, "So, where are you from?"

"Oklahoma."

"Really? How did you stumble across Cleveland State?"

"Distance, and my majors."

"Which are?"

"I'm double majoring – Art and Criminology."

"Hmm, maybe we shouldn't be friends. One of these days with a degree in criminology, you could be hunting me," he said jokingly.

Katie laughed. "Not if I can help it."

"What does that mean?"

"I don't think you want to do the family business. If that's the case, I'll be hunting your brother down, not you."

He chuckled. "You're bad."

She shrugged. "If you can't laugh about it, you'll probably be angry, right?"

"Yep." He paused. "Okay, here's the deal."

Katie raised an eyebrow at him in question.

"I like you and want to be your friend."

"Okayyyy. Why do I hear a *but* in there?"

"If we're friends, you have to promise to never arrest me."

Katie couldn't help the laughter on that one. "I don't think you're going to do it."

"Why not? Don't I seem like the boss type?"

"No, not really."

"Why not?"

"Because you have a heart."

*   *   *

It was a quiet walk between Seb and Katie as they made their way back to the dorm arm-in-arm. Finally, Seb couldn't take it anymore and questioned, "What's up between you and mafia boy?"

Giving him a look of warning, she asked, "What do you mean?"

"Why did you invite him to sit at your table?"

"Because he needs a friend."

"Not you," he said sternly. "Don't you think we've been through enough by losing Jillian? We don't want to lose you too."

"You won't lose me."

"Don't you get it?" he growled. "People end up dead around him."

Katie saw the passion and anger in his eyes. "I won't. I'm too smart."

"You will. You're naïve. You're like a child walking around on a nature preserve. If you don't pay attention, you'll get eaten alive."

She pulled her arm away from his. "Where do you get off calling me a child and saying I'm naïve?"

Seeing her look like a volcano about to blow, he knew he had to approach the rest of the conversation with caution. "I don't want to see you hurt. You're from a small town in Oklahoma. You like to see the best in people. That's not how the real world works. People can be evil. Jillian knew that all too well."

"Then why did she leave the library unaccompanied? You guys get upset at me for doing it and she did it too."

"The one and only time she did it, she was killed. Don't you think that would put the rest of us on edge? We love you, Katie. We don't want to see anything happen to you. Have you not noticed what all of the girls look like who have been attacked?"

"What do you mean?"

"Good grief!" He rolled his eyes. "They look like you and Jill. They have been tall, slender, and have long black hair."

"Their eye color isn't the same," she pointed out.

"It's dark when the sun goes down. Do you really think eye color has anything to do with it? You're studying criminology. You're smart. Are you saying you can't profile this guy by now? Be realistic. Go to your room and make a list. I'll bet you'll find more coincidences than you realize." He paused for a moment to let his words sink in before he went on, "Jill was a fighter. Her dad taught her well. Chances are that the guy wasn't expecting her to fight. My guess is that's why she's dead and the others who were attacked aren't."

"Are you saying she's dead because she fought back?"

"Had she let him rape her like he did the other girls, she would probably still be alive."

"Are you kidding me?" Katie stood there, furious. "So, as a woman, I'm just supposed to let a guy rape me so I can live?"

"Absolutely not! I'm saying she didn't let him, that's why he killed her."

Katie threw her hands in the air. "Unbelievable! That is the most –"

"I would rather you were never in that position to begin with. However, if it happens, fight back with everything you've got."

"But you said he could kill me."

"I think someone raping you would kill you on the inside anyway."

Katie stopped what was going to come out of her mouth and looked at him, dumbfounded.

He crouched so he was eye level with her and explained, "You are so far shut down, you barely cried at the funeral. Ethan said you cried the entire night you found Jillian, and after that it was like you shut your feelings off like a light switch. I'm afraid for you, Katie. If anything else happens, I'm afraid you'll shut down for good."

"What does this have to do with Giovanni?"

"His mother was killed because of who she was married to. Don't you think it would paint a double target on you if you were a friend to him *and* you look like the girls attacked? You are going to have to have body-guards around you twenty-four/seven at the rate you're going. That's not even pointing out the fact that you're currently living by yourself in a practically empty dorm. How is that supposed to make us comfortable? This is a terrifying situation for all of us."

"I'm only being a friend to him."

He let out a slow breath of air to keep himself under control. "Fine. Can you do it safely?"

"I don't understand. How can you safely be a friend to someone?"

"Use common sense and don't put yourself in a position that would put you in danger. Dom and Riccardo said I can walk you home from the diner. Please don't go out after sunset other than that."

"Are you kidding? You're asking me to be locked in the dorm from four o'clock in the afternoon until the next morning. I'm not a prisoner."

"I don't know how else to ensure your safety."

"You don't have to."

As he cautiously approached the arguing pair, the security officer asked, "Ready to go in your dorm?"

"Yes. Thank you. This conversation is finished," Katie said, glaring at Seb, daring him to say otherwise.

"At least think about it, will you? I would like to report to everyone that you're actually using your brain," Seb pleaded.

"Nice friend," the security officer quipped, unlocking the dorm door.

"Butt out," Seb snapped.

"If you're supposed to be her friend, I don't think calling her stupid would be a good thing."

"Who asked you?"

"Guys!" Katie grunted. "Ugh! Just let me in."

"Yes, ma'am," the security officer said, holding open the door. He waited for Seb to leave before he checked to make sure the door was locked and then left for the guard shack.

Katie slowly climbed the stairs, running the evening events through her mind. Seb's audacity shocked her, but then again so did Giovanni's tenderheartedness. She never imagined him to be so sweet.

She locked the door of the apartment behind her as she went in, and then went to her room and sat down on her bed, not sure what to do. That's when she looked toward her desk and saw her sketch-pad. She hadn't drawn in it since the week before the car accident on prom night. She had assignments for school, but the sketch pad on her desk was for personal use. She flipped to the last drawing she did. It was of the lake house. The group was there the week before prom for a fun weekend and to decorate for after the prom. She drew the scene from where she sat on the pier while the others were splashing around in the lake. She never wanted to forget the way the sun pierced through the trees, creating rainbows when the sun hit the sprays of water. She closed her eyes as she held the sketchpad to her chest, remembering the scents of the water and the natural woods. The squirrels chittering as they chased each other through the woods were drowned out by the roaring drone of the cicada bugs. Everyone, at that frozen moment in time, was happy.

She turned a couple pages back to the fiery furnace scene from her nightmare. She could almost see the images moving on the paper. The skinless hands were sticking out of the door, people begging for help, screaming and yelling in terror. As the fire danced around them, the people were burning, but were never consumed. She shuddered as she remembered the nightmare connected to it, and how the place reeked purely of death and devastation. There was no hope anywhere to be found in that realm. It represented a terrifying moment in time.

Going over to her window, she pushed it open. She felt closer to God when she talked to Him with the window open – no barriers between her and God. "Are you there? Look, I know You sent those agents here. At least I think I know that. I'm fairly sure You had me cross paths with Giovanni in the first place. I'm not sure why You let Jill die, though. She fought back. Was that a crime?" She sighed as she propped her chin on her hand. "I'm scared. I don't know if I will be alive tomorrow. You're starting to show me to trust the events before me. I'm asking You to show me that You will keep me safe. If I'm heading into the FBI, now is a good time to see if I'm cut out for it."

She sat down on her bed and turned to a fresh sheet of paper. She drew a picture of Giovanni before she drew pictures of each of her friends, all from the neck up, including Jillian. When she finished, she ran her fingers over Giovanni's picture. "I'll do it, only because it's not fair for anyone to be held prisoner by someone else."

*   *   *

Later that night around eight o'clock, she got a phone call in her room. "Hello?"

"Hey, Katie. It's Aaron," he responded. Aaron Sawyer was Jillian's boyfriend. He stood at only five-ten and had long black hair and brown eyes. He often got teased by his basketball buddies about his long hair, which he kept pulled back when he played for the school. Due to the rocker-style band he played the drums for, his lanky body was normally clothed in tight jeans, and sweaters or t-shirts, and black leather boots. Katie loved the fact that he rode an all-black Yamaha R6, which he often took Katie and Jillian for rides on.

"Hi, Aaron," she said, delighted to hear from him. She hadn't heard from him since the day of Jillian's funeral.

"You awake and decent?"

"Yeah," she said, confused. "Why?"

"I'm downstairs."

"Oh!" She threw open her window and looked down to see him on his cell phone at the front door. "I'll be down in a minute."

When she got down there, she quickly opened the door. "What are you doing out here?"

"Honestly?"

"You know me."

"Right." He nodded. "Honesty is always the key with you. Anyway, tomorrow is Christmas Eve."

"I see," Katie said as they took a seat on the couch down in the lobby. "Feeling a little lonely as the holidays approach?"

He sighed. "Yeah. It's not that I'm looking to fill the hole in my heart. I'm just looking for someone who understands my pain. I know you two were like sisters, so…"

"So, naturally, I would be one who would understand."

"Exactly," he said, relief evident on his face.

She rested her hand on his arm. "I do understand. If you need someone to talk to, you know I'm always here for you."

Sitting back on the couch, he looked a lot more relaxed, as he explained, "We had a concert last night and played her favorite song."

"How did you do?"

"I beat the tar out of the drums for that one. Bobby Lee reamed me for it later, but in the same sentence, praised the passion that came through. He said not to make it a habit. The kicker was that the audience was all over it."

"Cool!"

"Yes…and no. I shouldn't deviate from the way the set is laid out. I just couldn't help myself. Usually I can channel myself into my music, but I couldn't get all of the…." He snapped his fingers looking for the right word.

"Anger?" Katie offered.

"Exactly! I'm so angry, but I have nowhere to put it. I could play basketball, but I might accidently hurt someone. If I put all of my anger into the drums, I'll break them." He dropped his head into his hands. "I just don't know what to do."

"Is your motorcycle here?"

"Yeah. Why?"

"Because I think you need a ride. How about we take a ride and go get something to eat?"

He sighed, shaking his head. "Jilly used to do that for me when I was angry as well."

"You have a rough home life. You need an outlet. Just don't get me killed, though."

He chuckled. "If I get you killed, I'll kill myself. There is no way I am ever going to let anything happen to you. I would die first."

"While I appreciate that, I don't want anything to happen to you either."

"Go get your winter gear and let's go. I have an extra helmet."

Running upstairs, she grabbed her hat, coat, gloves, and scarf before heading back downstairs. She knew it would be a terribly cold ride, but Aaron needed her. She would do her best to keep him at a distance, though. She was aware of how much she and Jillian looked alike. She didn't want to take Jillian's place. Aaron wasn't her type anyway.

"Ready?" Katie asked, coming down the stairs.

"Yeah."

The Christmas lights flew by in streaks as they cruised around the downtown area for an hour before landing at a local restaurant down near the lake. "I know it will cost a bit for dinner here," Aaron said as they got off the bike, "but I appreciate you coming out with me."

"You should really save your money. How about we just get hot chocolate and dessert?"

"Sounds like a plan," he agreed.

After they were seated and enjoying their Boston cream pie and hot chocolate, Aaron asked, "Why aren't you dating Seb or Ethan?"

She just about spit out her hot chocolate, but forced it down. "What? Why?"

"Well, what's the reason?"

"Why?"

"Just curious. You're a sweet girl, they're nice guys…" he hinted.

She shrugged. "I like them, but I really don't want to go out with anyone right now."

"Why not?"

She thought about it for a moment before she responded, "I don't want to give up my goals for some guy."

"I don't think they would do that to you."

She shook her head. "I don't want to date them just yet. As a matter of fact, I told them to date other girls. I think they should be happy."

"What if they're happy with you?"

She slowly chewed the bite of pie in her mouth before swallowing. "I guess I don't want to lose myself in a relationship."

"What do you mean by that?" he asked, sincerely interested.

She thought for a moment on how to express her feelings. "Sometimes when you are with someone and doing so much together, you lose your own identity."

"I see." He pondered her words. "I think that could be my problem."

"Why do you say that?"

"Because I feel as if a part of me is missing. I loved Jillian. We did a lot together and were together for almost five years.

I'm telling you right now…if I ever find out who killed her, they won't need to worry about a trial."

"What? Why?"

He narrowed his eyes, as he stated with pure hatred, "They won't make it to trial. I'll kill them first."

*   *   *

Katie woke up the next morning to see that a blizzard had hit the campus overnight. The wind created snow drifts already topping four-feet tall as the snow continued to fall. "Good grief!" Katie exclaimed in shock. "I'm going to get snowed in and I don't have any food!"

She quickly dressed before it got too much later. The small grocery store a block from campus opened at nine o'clock. Since the snow was deep, she knew she couldn't drive. By the time she walked there, the store would be open and she could get back quickly.

She called security to let them know she was going to the store. The security officer agreed to meet her back at the dorm in an hour and a half. By her calculations, that would give her enough time to get what she needed.

The wind about knocked her over as soon as she set foot outside her dorm. "Seriously?" she said, pulling her coat tighter around her body. It didn't matter how bundled she was though, cold was still cold, and the winter weather Lake Erie kicked off could be wicked cold.

"Come in, come in, child," the store owner, Erich Berliner, said with his thick German accent. He and his wife, Elena, owned and operated the small convenient store. He opened the door for Katie when he saw her crossing the parking lot, bundled to the hilt. "What are you doing out here? We almost didn't open."

"I'm sorry," she said, brushing off the snow. "I should have done it yesterday, but I was preoccupied. I need to get some food to make it through at least Christmas. The café won't be open on that day."

"I see. And," he glanced out at the parking lot, "where's your car?"

"I walked. The snow's too deep to drive."

"Ahhh, not if you have four-by-four," he gestured toward his truck. "However," he glanced back outside, "I'll probably close after you finish. I don't think there will be too many people venturing outside today if they're smart."

"I'll hurry," she said and grabbed a cart. She would have to keep her load light, but healthy.

The first thing she picked up was a gallon of milk. "So much for light," she said to herself.

"What are you looking for?" Erich asked, meeting her in the middle of the second aisle.

"I don't know. I guess I can get stuff for chicken and dumplings."

"Sounds like a good choice. Thick and hearty is always good on a cold day."

"Right." She picked up the ingredients, along with some fresh fruits and vegetables. She also got what she needed to make a vegetable dip so she could snack on the vegetables whenever she wanted.

"What about some cereal for breakfast?" Erich suggested.

"Actually, I usually have crunchy peanut butter toast and orange juice," she explained, and retrieved those as well before she went to the cash register.

"Tell ya what," Erich said at the register, "Give me a twenty and we'll call it good."

"Can you do that?" Katie asked in shock.

"It's my store. I don't want to waste time weighing all of those fruits and veggies. It's a bitter cold day. Do me a favor and get home and stay there. And, have a Merry Christmas."

"Will do," she said, handing him a twenty. "And, thank you. Merry Christmas to you, too."

"I'm headed home myself. Oh, and here. I know they're your favorite," he said, handing her a package of mint chocolate cookies.

"Thank you so much! Please pass my Christmas blessings to your family. Be careful on your way home," she said and double-bagged her groceries into plastic bags as Erich turned the lights off. Balancing all of the bags in her hands, she pushed open the doors. "Oh no!" she exclaimed as the wind cut through all the way to her skin, sending a chill up her spine.

"Need a ride?"

She looked up to see Nick standing there, leaning on his car with his arms crossed. When she did, she dropped three of the bags, one of which included the milk. "Great!" she huffed and brushed the hair that fell in her face out of the way.

"Here, let me help you. It's too dangerous to walk in this blizzard," he offered, picking up the dropped bags.

"If it's so dangerous, what are you doing out here?"

"Making sure you're not going to freeze to death. C'mon, let's get you to your dorm," he said, setting the bags in the back seat.

"Well, if you can't trust the FBI, who can you trust," she said and set her bags in the back seat as well. When she got in the passenger's side of his dark navy blue 4x4 Ford Explorer with grey leather seats, she was surprised by the warmth of the seat.

"I turned the heaters on so it would be warm when you got in," he mentioned, putting the truck into drive. "So, I reckon we have t' stop by security on the way in?"

She glanced at her watch. "Yeah, they're not supposed to be at the dorm for another half hour."

"I see. Not a problem," he said, pulling out of the parking lot onto the deserted streets. Outside of the salt trucks and plows, there were few cars who dared to go out into the severe weather.

What normally would have been a five-minute drive took them fifteen minutes to get to the gate house. The security officer said he would meet them down at the dorm in a few minutes before he let them onto the campus.

While they waited, Nick turned on his Australian charm. "So, what's a nice girl like you doin' out here in this bitter cold weather?"

"Food is a necessity."

"An', why didn't you already have it?"

"Because I have been too busy changing rooms and getting unpacked."

After another minute, Nick asked, "So, have you thought about what we talked about yesterday?"

"You mean about Giovanni?"

"Yep."

"I have," she admitted.

"And?"

"I think he needs a friend."

"Are you going to be that friend?"

Katie debated in her head how to answer.

"Are you going to be that friend?" he asked again after a minute of silence.

"Depends."

"On what?"

"On how this is going to work?"

"Well," Nick considered his words carefully, "if you're going to be his friend, along with keeping your eyes and ears open for us, then I'll look after you and be your handler."

"Meaning?"

"Meaning you report to me and me only. If you see or hear anything that strikes you as something we may want to know, you contact me."

"How will you keep me safe?"

"You're just a friend." He shrugged. "What's so dangerous about being a friend?"

"What if I feel threatened?"

"Then you contact me and we'll handle it from there."

"Will changing my identity have anything to do with keeping me safe?"

"Potentially," he admitted.

She debated in her head for another moment before she said, "Okay. I'll trust you."

"Thank you," he said relieved. After a minute, he asked, "Want me to let you into your dorm?"

"You can do that?"

"How do you think we got in before?"

"I guess I never thought about it."

They got out and he carried most of the bags to the door. He set them down for only a moment before he swiftly picked the lock.

"Wow! Can you show me how to do that?"

"Someday," he agreed, picking up the bags. "In the meantime, let's get these up to your apartment."

"Thank you," she said, grateful for the help. She could have managed the walk home if she had to, but she was glad he was there.

He set the bags on the counter. "So, Christmas is tomorrow. Are you ready?"

"What's to get ready?"

He looked at her in confusion. "Do you not celebrate it?"

"It's not that. I don't have anyone to celebrate it with."

"What about with your dad? Didn't you celebrate it growing up?"

"Not really."

"Wow. Christmas growin' up with our clan was huge."

"I'll have to take your word for it," she said, putting the fruit and vegetables, along with the milk on her shelf of the refrigerator. She left out some chicken to thaw before marking the rest and put it into the freezer. She also marked her bread and peanut butter before placing them in her cupboard.

"Why aren't you going home for break?"

"I don't want to."

"Why haven't you gone home since moving out here?"

Stunned, she asked, "How do you know that?"

"I'm FBI." He shrugged. "I know a lot. We wouldn't have asked you for help without checking you out thoroughly first."

"Really? What else do you know?"

"Someday I'll tell you."

She huffed. "Yeah, right."

"Are you going to be okay in here alone?"

"Yes. Why?"

"Just making sure. It's eerily quiet," he said, catching every sound.

"Meh." She shrugged. "It lets me think."

After a moment, he mentioned, "I don't see any Christmas decorations."

"I don't have any Christmas decorations. My apartment mates took theirs down before they left because they didn't want to take them down when they returned."

"I see." He paused, looking around again. "You know it's Christmas Eve, right?"

She laughed. "Why are you so stuck on Christmas?"

"Because I won't let you spend Christmas without a single present or a tree."

"Really?" She crossed her arms as she leaned on the counter. "And, how are you going to do that?"

"We're going shopping."

"In this blizzard? Don't you have a job to do?"

"I do. Fortunately for me, you're a large portion of it for now. C'mon, let's go shoppin'."

"I don't have the money for that."

"Oh, really?" he challenged. "Have I told you I work for FBI?"

She grunted in frustration. "Fine. Let's go." She snagged her coat, gloves, and scarf off the chair and they headed out of the dorm. When they got to the car, a thought struck her. "Wasn't the security officer supposed to be down here to let me in?"

"He's one of ours."

She got in the car and buckled. "What do you mean 'one of ours'?"

"Our guys are posing as security for this break. There is at least one of us on per shift. So, when you call them, they call me."

"Are you telling me our crack-pot security staff is made of FBI agents?"

"The main ones are, yes. The other ones on shift aren't."

"What would you guys have done had I said 'no'?"

"We're here for a different reason. Stumbling onto you was just a bonus."

"What reason are you here for?"

"Director Shaw's daughter was killed, that makes it our case."

"I see."

"And, I don't reckon they would take kindly to being called crack-pot security." He chuckled.

She studied him for a few moments while they drove. Noting his strikingly handsome features and his bulky body, along with his fascinating accent, she realized why he was the one assigned to her. "I'll bet you really attract the ladies," she baited him.

He chuckled again. "You're funny."

"And you're obvious."

Startled by her response, he glanced at her before going back to the road. "What do you mean by that?"

"Why did they assign you to me? Was it that they thought your good looks and Aussie charm would get me to work with you?"

He didn't answer.

"Well, allow me to clear something up for you."

"By all means."

"I'm not doing this for you. I'm doing this for Giovanni."

"Meaning?"

"Meaning he and I had a talk. You're right. He doesn't want anything to do with his father's business. I'm in it to help him achieve his dream and live in peace."

"What does that mean?"

"It means that it wouldn't matter who was assigned to me, I would still do it. I'm immune to your charm and couldn't care less about your good looks. I look deeper."

"And, you haven't been able to find someone whose heart you find attractive in two and a half years?"

"I have. I'm just not interested in dating them until I graduate."

"Why?"

"Because I want to graduate and get my degree. I don't want to be reliant on anyone but myself."

"What about God?"

"What *about* Him?"

"I know you go to church…well, let me rephrase that. I know you *used* to go to church. Why don't you go here?"

"Wow," she said, sitting back in her seat with her arms crossed.

He smirked in satisfaction. "I sense a little hostility in you."

"You sense a little 'why doesn't he mind his own business?' in me," she corrected.

"Hey. If you don't want to, that's your prerogative. I'm only sayin' you used to go. What happened?"

"Stacey and I are working on it."

"I would think you would have reached the point of being done with *working on it* and would be *going* by now. What are you waiting for?"

"This is fixin' to be a long day if we don't stop arguing."

"Fixin' to?"

She huffed and then corrected her wording, "Going to."

"Who said we were arguing?"

"I don't care for you."

"Why not?"

"Because you are conceited and think you know better."

"Judgmental much?"

"Arrogant much?"

"Hmmm, seems Simmons might have underestimated you."

"Really? What was his assessment?"

"He thought you would fall for me – hook, line, and sinker."

Katie burst out in laughter.

"Okay, now I'm offended."

"I should be the one offended. Did he really think I was that easy?"

"Well," he shrugged and slightly blushed, "it usually works that way."

"Not this time, kangaroo boy."

He glanced at her for a moment before he asked, "Do you like Giovanni?"

"What is with you and my relationships?"

"Just curious."

"No, I only like him for a friend."

"Do you have a boyfriend?"

"Don't you know that?"

"Why would I ask if I knew?"

"I thought you had this massive file on me."

"Wow." He whistled. "A challenge. I like you."

"Good."

"Good what?"

"Now you know where we stand."

"Which is?"

"That I'm not going to fall for you. I don't care what you think. I'm not doing this for you. Also, that I'm only going to keep you around to keep me safe. Otherwise you can go fly a kite for all I care."

He couldn't help the laughter that escaped his mouth. "Tell me what you really think."

"You don't *want* to know what I really think."

"Why not?"

"Because you seem to think I'm so shallow that I would fall for you. That's insulting."

"No worries. I'll pass that along to Simmons."

"Good. Now that we know where we stand, would you like to start over?" she asked.

He debated for a few moments before he relented. "Okay." He stuck his hand out. "G'day, I'm Nick Locke. I'm goin' t' be your handler for this case."

"Hello, Agent Locke," she said, shaking his hand.

"Please, call me Nick."

"All right, Nick. You can call me Miss MacKenna."

"Oh boy," he laughed, "this is going to be fun."

Chapter 3

On Thin Ice

When they finished shopping, Nick helped Katie carry everything upstairs before he left to go home. The storm had picked up a bit, making it dangerous for even his four-by-four.

After setting up the three-foot Christmas tree with various country-themed decorations, and white and blue lights in her room, she decided to decorate the rest of the room as well. Around the ceiling of her room, she hung a couple strings of white lights, creating an artsy design on the ceiling. This gave a softer feel to the otherwise fluorescent lights and stark white walls. Hanging some of her drawings, along with a message board on her door for when her apartment mates returned, gave the room the life it was lacking.

Working diligently, she lost track of time until she heard the buzzer go off around four-thirty that evening for her dorm. When the dorm is closed, it is still possible to ring a buzzer to let people know someone is at the door.

She poked her head out the window to see Giovanni standing there. "Hey!" she called down to him.

He looked up, shielding his eyes from the floodlights and snowfall. "Hey. Do you want a ride to the café?"

"Yep. Be down in a minute," she said and closed her room window. A thrill of excitement ran through her while she bundled for the bitter cold. She had to admit he was cute, but she forced herself to not look at him that way. That was not why she was being his friend. She was going to help him escape the prison without bars that his father created for him. She wanted to free him. "What brings you out here?"

"Your safety," he said, putting his arm out for her. As she looped her arm through his, he clarified, "I couldn't imagine you walking by yourself to the café in this blizzard."

"Really?"

"I don't mean to offend you, but I am too much of a gentleman to let you do that without at least offering to drive you over." He gestured toward his red Jeep Rubicon.

"That'll work," she agreed. "And, being a gentleman seems to be a lost art."

"Not with my family. My father insists on it."

"Good for him."

"So," he opened her door for her to climb in before he ran around to his side and got in as well, "Do you want to go to the café or somewhere else?"

"I don't think much else is open. Let's just head to the café. I know they'll be looking for me, and if I'm not there Seb will pitch a fit."

He chuckled. "Yeah, I could see that. He's very protective of you. By the way, I never properly thanked you for standing up for me yesterday."

"No problem. I figure if your dad does what you say he does, then you more than likely don't have many friends."

"I don't."

"Then it's my privilege to be your friend."

"Really?"

"Yes."

He grinned as he said, "That's the best Christmas present anyone has ever given me."

Katie smiled to herself. She never imagined being someone's friend would give her so much joy and satisfaction. That's when she got a twinge of guilt. *Would being his friend and helping him out of the 'family business' cause her to lose his friendship? Her intention was to help him, not set him up.* She cemented in her mind at that moment to keep her intentions pure.

"Um, looks like the café is closed," Giovanni said as they turned the corner toward the café. He pulled into the empty parking lot to see the building completely dark.

"I would think Seb would have called me if it was closed," Katie said, upset. She turned to Giovanni and said, "Please take me back to the dorm. We'll eat there."

"That may not be wise. With not a lot of people in your dorm, I don't want you to feel the least bit uncomfortable in our friendship."

"Then, what are you going to eat for dinner?"

"I'll eat at home. I'll make sure you get to your dorm safely first, though."

"I have to say I've never met a guy who was as much a gentleman as you are being. You are unpresumptuous, yet confident. Those are very admirable qualities."

"Thanks," he said, sheepishly.

"Why haven't you dated before?"

"That would require being a friend to someone who is near my age and not packing heat."

"I see. And now that you have a friend like that?"

"Well, I don't want to lose the friendship. I value it too much."

"Good, because I'm not looking for anything except a friendship either."

When they pulled up to security, the officer poked his head out the gatehouse window. "Wicked night for you guys to be out. I don't remember getting a call from you either," he hinted.

"Sorry about that. He gave me a ride," Katie explained.

"I see," he said and walked to open the gate. "Be careful, the roads are ice. I'll radio my partner to let you into the dorm."

"Yes, sir," Giovanni acknowledged before pulling onto the campus. "Are you sure you want to go in there by yourself? I have an uneasy feeling."

"I'll be fine."

"If you're sure."

"I'll be fine. We haven't been gone long enough for anything to have happened. It's okay. I feel bad you drove all the way out here for nothing."

"I'll tell you what. If it'll make you feel better, I'll stay and play a game with you before I go so you won't feel bad," he offered.

"Let me make you dinner and we have a deal."

"Somehow I knew you would get your way. You have a deal," he said, shaking her hand as she had a satisfied smile on her face.

After he parked the jeep behind the dorm, they carefully maneuvered their way up the slick walkways to the door, where they were met by the security officer. "Is he going in too?" he asked.

"Yes. He'll be staying for a couple of hours to play a game and eat dinner," Katie explained, knowing he would pass the information on to Nick.

"If you need us, you know where we are. I'll check back in a couple of hours to make sure you're okay."

Katie smiled in appreciation as he let them in, locking the door behind them.

"They seem protective of you, too," Giovanni observed. "Why is it people seem so protective of you?"

"Because we lost Jillian only a couple of weeks ago and no one wants to lose anyone else."

"I see." He thought for a moment before he asked, "Are you afraid of me?"

"Me?" she snickered. "Afraid of you? No."

He chuckled at her laughter. "Why not? I'm a mafia leader's son."

"But you're not part of the mafia."

"I am by name, which means you're hanging out with the mafia by association," he pointed out as they entered her apartment.

Ignoring his last comment, she went to her room and returned with a deck of cards. "Wanna play a little Texas Hold 'em?"

"Texas Hold 'em? How do you play that?"

"It's a revised version of poker. Look it up on your cell phone and study it while I make chicken and dumplings," she said, and proceeded to start cooking.

As the heavenly scent of chicken and dumplings filled the air, Giovanni's stomach growled. He was hungrier than he thought. He would periodically glance up at Katie in amazement. She seemed easy going, yet had that strong Irish temper. She reminded him a lot of his mother – a full-blooded Irish girl, who married an Italian. Under normal circumstances that would be a volatile combination, but his mother seemed to have a balance to her temperament. Katie had it too.

He sighed as he continued to read about the game. "You're an enigma."

Katie laughed. "What?"

"You're Irish, but also laid back. My mother was Irish and was the same way. My grandparents, on the other hand, were true Irish. My grandfather would frequent the pub, and my grandmother would beat him on the head with the iron skillet when he got home while she gave him what for. Don't even ask me about my full-blooded Italian grandparents. Let's just say it caused quite a stir in their families when they got married."

"I'm sure. My dad sounds like your grandfather. Not sure how my mother dealt with him before she passed. I was only seven when she died."

"While my dad was the boss of the house, my mom somehow brought out a softer side to his rough exterior. That has seemed to diminish since her passing."

"Shame. I would think he would only want the best for you."

"Oh, he does…as long as it fits his plan."

"I don't understand."

"That's okay, neither do I," he said, and shoved his thoughts back to Texas Hold 'em. He was a good poker player, but she was right, this had a different spin to it. He was sure he would be able to figure it out within a couple of hands. It didn't look too difficult. He looked back up at Katie, admiring the way she floated around the kitchen. "Do you like to cook?"

"I do, but I have a limited selection of things I *can* cook, sorry to say," she admitted.

"I would think it would be easy."

The phone in her room rang. "Excuse me. I have to get that. It could be security checking to make sure you haven't killed me yet." She winked before she left the room. He laughed, taking it in stride, the way she intended. "Hello?" she answered the phone.

"Ya know, I'm not sure whether to come down there and kick your behind or not!" Ethan growled over the phone.

Katie burst out in laughter. "I see you've talked to Seb."

"Katie, this isn't funny!"

"He's harmless. As a matter of fact, since the café is closed, he's eating here with me –"

"Katie Marie MacKenna!" Ethan exploded. Katie's eyes widened in surprise as he ranted, "You have *got* to be kidding me! I was calling to wish you a Merry Christmas, but now I'm furious! How can you seriously be eating dinner with mafia boy alone in your dorm? Do you have a death wish? I don't – I don't even know what to say to that."

"Sounds like quite a mouthful right there," Katie quipped in irritation. She did not like being berated, no matter who it was.

"I have half a mind to drive down there tonight and bring you back home with me, kicking and screaming if I have to!"

"Yeah, good luck with that."

He took a couple of deep breaths to settle himself before he started again, this time calmer, "Why can't you understand the choices you make could get you killed? You are skating on thin ice here."

"I'll be okay."

"You hope. I only hope you're still there when I get back after break. You are seriously scaring me to death up here. I feel like calling the others and making one of them get you and hold you down until I can get there."

"You're not my dad."

"No, I'm not. I'm your friend, and a close one at that, who is afraid for your safety. We buried your roommate before break and I don't want to bury you after."

"I'll be fine."

"Sure," he said with sarcasm dripping all over his voice, "you're just hanging out with a crime family…nothing to worry about there. He's *perfectly* safe to be around." He paused. "Have we told you people end up *dead* around him?"

"With an attitude like that, no wonder he doesn't have any friends."

"Oh, for crying out loud! I can't do this. I have to call you later. I'm too angry to talk right now. I love you, Katie, but I have to go."

"I love you, too. If I don't talk to you tomorrow have a Merry Christmas."

"Just be safe, please? Make smart choices?"

"I will. I'm safer than you think."

He sighed. "I love you, Katie, and hope to someday take you out on a date, but I can't do that if you're dead."

"I'm fine. I will be fine. I'll see you when you return."

"All right," he relented. "I know better than to argue with that Irish temper of yours. It can send a chill deeper within you than even Lake Erie can dish out."

"Love you. Gotta go."

"Love you, too. Bye," he said and hung up.

"Sounded like a serious conversation," Giovanni remarked, as he looked up from his phone when she walked back out to the kitchen.

She waved him off. "Just a concerned friend."

"You're probably going to get more of those calls. Hanging out with me seems to have that effect."

"Trust me. There are worse people I could be hanging out with."

"Really? Like who?"

"Your brother," she said, and he burst out in laughter.

"That is true."

*   *   *

When Giovanni left a couple of hours later, Katie got a call from the gate making sure she was okay. After that, she went to bed, feeling perfectly comfortable in her decision to be his friend. Her other friends may be pitching a fit, but she knew something they didn't. She knew the FBI was keeping an eye on her. She also knew God had a hand in this as well, and He was more powerful than anything. This would be the testing ground. She would either pass with flying colors or it would be an epic fail. She would have to let things play out to see what the final verdict would be.

*   *   *

"Hail! Hail! All hail to the victors!" Claire cheered when Seth, Nick, Dakota, and Todd walked in from a successful bust. Unfortunately, it happened at the inopportune time of around six o'clock on Christmas morning, so they were a bit punchy from lack of sleep and the rush of adrenaline. While the guys were in the field, Claire and Emma kept an eye on things from the office.

Emma clapped and whistled. "Great job, guys."

"Yeah, one down, another four hundred and sixty-two to go," Dakota said, taking a seat at his desk to write the report.

"I would think you would be happy. It was your snitch who gave the info for the bust," Nick pointed out, sitting down on the corner of Dakota's desk.

Dakota stood to his full six-foot-two height. He leaned on the desk, glaring at Nick with his dark-brown eyes blazing. "Diane paid dearly for that information. She will be in the ICU for days before they can get her stabilized enough to move her to a regular room."

Nick stood and crossed his arms, making him look even more bulky than he was. "Back that Italian bravado down several notches, mate. Diane would be happy at what we accomplished today. Taking out four Rodchenko members was a way to pay them back for what they did to her."

"They were low-level pond scum and you know it. If we held off, we would have gotten further up the food chain."

"We'll get them," he said, confidently. "Katie will get us some useful information."

"Oh, you think your little Irish princess over there is going to really get us something we can use?" Todd chuckled, shaking his head.

"What's that supposed to mean?"

"You didn't see her last night when they went to her dorm."

"He went to her dorm?"

"For a couple of *hours*," Todd hinted. "Doesn't take a rocket scientist to figure that one out. She's a pretty girl, he's a nice looking guy…it was bound to happen."

Nick shook his head. "She wouldn't do that."

"Oh no?" Claire jumped into the conversation, taking the opportunity to give Katie's reputation another hit. "I'm sorry, have you been on a college campus lately? I was against this from the start. Seriously, how can you trust a child to do a trained professional's job? Her mind isn't on the job at hand. It's on the hot looking guy she was with in a practically empty dorm for at least two hours. Unbelievable!" She threw her hands in the air. "How are we going to explain to Diane that we sent a child in to get information on the Rodchenko and Rossi families?"

"Why would we have to?" Seth questioned in irritation. "This is *my* team. I don't answer to Diane. I answer to Director

Shaw and he approved it. He has faith in Katie. We need to as well."

"You guys are *so* blind," Claire breathed out, shuffling her paperwork.

"Jealous?" Nick observed.

"Jealous? Why would I be jealous?"

"Because young Miss MacKenna has the admiration, approval, and support of not only a senior agent from the Washington DC office, but of our very own Director Shaw, and he didn't send you in."

"Why would he?"

"Because when we send in undercover for young people, it's usually you, but Director Shaw overrode that. He took the opportunity to bring in new blood."

"And, if it works out, I may snag her once she finishes her two year stint with the police," Seth pointed out.

Claire narrowed her eyes at him. "You wouldn't dare!"

Nick smirked in satisfaction. "What? Feeling your territory being infringed upon?"

"The only thing she's going to be looking at is you guys," she said, upset at the prospect. "She can't be watching your backs if she's watching your –"

"Claire!" Seth stood up in shock. "That's enough! We have the utmost confidence in her. Now, if you want to continue this conversation, I'll be happy to do it in Director Shaw's office when he gets in."

"She won't be looking at us in that way anyway." Nick shook his head. "She doesn't like me."

"Morning, folks," Brenda Birch from personnel walked into the room with a lady about thirty-five years old. "I have a new temp for your receptionist. Her name is Carrie Fielding. Be nice to her. She's here today to fill out paperwork and will be starting tomorrow."

"Is she going to do her job?" Seth asked. The office tended to flip through receptionists faster than Seth could remember their names.

"I'm sure she will. Just be nice."

"Welcome, that will be your desk," Seth gestured toward the empty receptionist desk by the office door. "Key thing to remember is even if we're sitting right here, we're not here. Tell them we're working on a break in the case and take a message."

"Got it," Carrie said before she and Brenda disappeared once again.

"What do you mean she doesn't like you?" Emma asked when they were gone.

"Well, it seems she thinks I'm arrogant and egotistical."

"Seriously?" Dakota chuckled. "I like this girl."

"Yeah, she's the first one we've seen not succumb to your charm. Either you're losing your touch, or –"

"No, she reads people very well. I *was* being arrogant," Nick cut Todd off. "She called me on it."

"Hmm, she's smarter than we thought," Seth said, now reconsidering his decision to include Katie. He was banking on her falling for Nick so she wouldn't get too close to Giovanni.

Chapter 4

Ice Queen

Christmas morning, Katie woke to the deafening silence that had surrounded her for the past few weeks. She strolled out to the kitchen, made her peanut butter toast, and poured a glass of orange juice before she headed down to the game room to watch the Christmas Day parade. While traditions in her home were limited, that was one she enjoyed. She fondly remembered watching them with her mother on the couch while her dad made pecan waffles for breakfast after they opened the presents. After her mother passed, the only tradition that stood was a present or two and the parade, which she watched by herself.

After the parade, she cleaned up, got dressed, and grabbed her sketch pad. She called security to tell them she was going to take a walk. They agreed to meet her back at the dorm in a couple of hours. In the meantime, she would have her hot chocolate in a thermos to keep her warm while she drew.

The storm eased some time in the night after blasting the area throughout the entire day before, leaving the sun to break through the clouds. The light glistened off the snow like glitter, while the wind let the fresh layer of snow blow around in wisps. The tallest drift she saw topped at six feet, but was as low as three feet. They got a lot of snow from this last blizzard and the wind continued to bounce the flakes through the air as it silently floated along the air stream.

Her footprints being the first in the newly fallen snow, peaceful and serene were the only words that came to mind. "Christmas snow is the best," Katie sighed, sweeping the snow off the bench next to the pond with her gloved hands before sitting down. Opening her sketch pad, she was armed with five pencils for this trip. Sketching the scene before her, she lost herself in the tranquility around her, completely oblivious to anyone else.

*   *   *

Dakota walked over the top of the hill to see Katie near the pond. She sat cross-legged on the bench with a thermos next to her and a sketch pad on her lap in front of her. Drawing seemed to center her. Dakota shook his head. The only thing that centered him was a good raid. In his twenty-six years of life, he had never been able to achieve the level of peace he saw on Katie's face at that moment. Knowing the storms that surrounded her, he was dumbfounded as to how she did it.

"Where is she?" Nick asked.

"Over there." Dakota gestured toward her. "She's been here for about forty-five minutes already. It's weird."

"What's weird?"

"She lost her roommate about two weeks ago, she's befriended an organized crime boss's son, has several friends ticked off at her, yet here she sits, looking like she doesn't have a care in the world. I have to admit I'm kind of envious."

Nick smiled. "If only things were that black and white."

"How does she do that? She hasn't even moved."

"She's in her own little world."

"And that doesn't concern you?"

"Would I be here if I wasn't concerned?"

"You know it's Christmas, right?"

"Yep."

"I know you don't have family around, but don't you have some girl you could be spending Christmas with?"

"I am. I'm spending it with my charge," he said, gesturing to Katie. "The rest of my family is in Australia or Montana. As far as a girl? Not at the moment. You have family to be spending it with, though."

"Yeah. Todd and I have split today. I get off duty at three and then he takes over."

"I see. Well," he patted Dakota's chest, "I got this one, mate. You can head back to that pathetic excuse for a guard shack now."

"Really? Am I being dismissed? Shouldn't I at least introduce myself to her?"

"And have her first impression of 'Mr. Metro' be you in a rent-a-cop suit? She's already called you blokes crackpot security. I don't think you want her remembering you in that."

"Good point," he nodded. He scratched his chest as he mentioned, "Polyester makes me break out in hives. I'll be glad when this assignment is over."

"It's going to be a while before you can get back to wearing your designer suits on a permanent basis again. Getting a son to flip on his father is not an overnight thing."

He turned and studied Katie for a few moments before he asked, "Are you guys sure she's capable of a task this big?"

"With me by her side, how could she miss?"

"Yeah. Egotistical and arrogant. She called that one right." Dakota patted his shoulder before he left for the gate house.

While Dakota disappeared over the hill, Nick continued to watch Katie. He leaned on a tree with his arms crossed, watching her draw. The intensity and focus with which she worked was refreshing. Nick had seen some of her drawings before, and understood focus was demanded with such talent. Her drawings were crisp and clear, like a black and white photograph. They were detailed beyond belief.

As he watched the way the sun lit her jet-black hair, it made him catch his breath. The wind blew by her, slightly rustling the curls at the end of the layers. Her face seemed to glow at the suns reflection with her pale skin, and it made the rosiness of her cheeks stand out even more. He had seen her move, graceful and smooth, like an angel.

A mini avalanche of snow fell from the tree above, sending a portion of it down his back. "All right, already," he said as he flipped the snow off his coat, and shuddered when a piece of it slid down his spine. "I'm going."

When he walked up to the bench, Katie noticed the movement out of the corner of her eye. "Morning, Agent Locke," she greeted him.

"You can call me Nick."

Gesturing to a spot on the bench beside her, she invited him, "Okay, Nick, have a seat."

Using his gloves, he cleared the snow that had blown onto the bench since she sat down, and took his seat. "Can I see?"

When she handed him the sketch pad, he let out a low whistle. "You have an amazing talent. I couldn't draw like this if my life depended on it."

"Thank you. It's my way of escape."

"What are you escaping?"

Katie didn't answer. She remained transfixed on the scene before her.

"Are you escaping your friends? Mainly Ethan?" he probed.

She furrowed her brow. "How do you know about that?"

"We have your phone tapped," he said, nonchalantly. Noting the anger and shock that visibly rang through her body when she stiffened, he explained, "It's for your protection. And, at this moment in time, we're bugging your apartment and room as well."

"I didn't give you permission to do that," she said, mortified.

"You don't have to. You working for us and having Giovanni Rossi in your apartment last night concerned us, so we got permission this morning to bug your apartment. As far as the phone, we did that as soon as you said you would befriend Giovanni."

"Are you serious? For how long?"

"As long as we need."

She shuddered. "I don't want to go back to my room. That's just creepy."

"I would think it would be a relief."

"Really? Is your apartment bugged? Do you have people around you watching everything you do, not knowing who they are?"

"They've been there the whole time. Why are you getting freaked out now? This is part and parcel in working with and for the FBI."

She crossed her arms. "Fine. Doesn't mean I have to like it."

"What are you, two?" He scoffed.

She reached down and grabbed a pile of snow. Quickly forming it into a ball, she threw it as hard as she could at Nick.

"What was that for?" he asked, shoving the snow off his black leather coat.

With a sly smile, she slowly lowered her hand down to the snow and scooped another handful.

"Don't you dare!" He jumped off the bench with a smile on his face, leaving the sketch pad in his seat.

She shoved a handful of snow at him, spraying his face and coat.

"Oh, you're going to get it if you don't stop," he warned, wiping the snow off his face.

Slinking off the bench, she went around the back, filling both hands with snow. She threw it at him…and it was on!

At first he took mercy on her, being a girl and all. After several more double-handed throws, though, she was fair game. He would duck behind a tree for cover and then let the snow fly with his eyes closed, due to the snow that almost seemed to be continuously flying in his direction.

To him, she seemed to be everywhere. After ten minutes, he ran for another tree, only to get machine gunned by snow. He ducked behind the tree and peeked around the other side to see that both Dakota and Todd, at some point, had joined Katie in the snowball fight.

"That's not fair!" he shouted.

The trio burst out in laughter. "Took you long enough," Dakota said. "And you call yourself an FBI agent. She's good, but not *that* good."

"Three against one is just not right."

"But your size against tiny, little ol' me, is?" Katie countered.

"You're not all that tiny." He peeked around the tree, only to get a barrage of snowballs thrown at him. "Not fair!"

"She is like half your size," Todd pointed out. "We add the element of fairness to it."

"Make it *one* of you and her, and it will be fair," Nick offered.

"Fair enough," Todd agreed. "I'll go protect the sketch pad on the bench while I officiate."

Dakota questioned, "A referee? For a snowball fight?"

"More like an announcer," Todd corrected, and headed over to the bench. He cleaned the snow off the sketch pad and bench, and took his seat. "Here we are, today, folks, down at Cleveland State University, where the two final teams will battle it out."

"Seriously," Dakota snickered, "You sound like a sports announcer."

"If it wasn't the FBI, I would be in communications," Todd explained.

"I would think communications would be safer," Katie said as she stacked the snow into a pile of snowballs.

"Maybe, but the FBI is more fun and rewarding. Wouldn't trade it for the world. Now," he got back into his announcer voice, "This is the final battle of the season. It's pretty boy, Dakota Wolfe, and the Ice Queen, Katie MacKenna. Don't let their good looks fool you, both are ferociously competitive and are only looking for blood. Meanwhile, on the other side of the field, is the one-man team of Nick Locke. He's the Thunder from Down Under…and this Aussie doesn't like to lose. Who will win this battle? Your guess is as good as mine. Let the games begin!" He shouted, and the snow went flying.

For over an hour they ducked behind trees and statues, while they stocked snowballs or used them in rapid succession. Just when Katie was about to give up, Nick came from around a tree with his hands in the air, "I give."

"Good!" Dakota said aloud. Then in a quieter voice, he added, "I wasn't sure how much longer I was going to be able to last. My fingers are red."

"Mine too. I was about to give up."

"Don't tell him that. We'll never hear the end of him winning two-to-one."

"No doubt," Katie agreed. "That's why I fought as long I could."

As they slowly made their way over to Todd and Nick, Drew mentioned, "Ya know, he's not as bad as he seems. He's a nice guy once you get to know him."

"You mean underneath all that bravado and arrogance, and I mean *deep* down, there's a real gentleman in there?"

Dakota laughed as he rested his hand on her shoulder. "Yep, I like you. We need to keep you around more often. There aren't too many people who can humble the Thunder from Down Under."

Nick kept an eye on Dakota and Katie as they slowly walked toward him and Todd. He felt a twinge of jealousy when Dakota put his hand on her shoulder. She looked like a cold, drown rat, soaked head to toe with the snow…but still, there was something about her that intrigued him.

Todd chuckled. "She *really* doesn't like you."

"What makes you say that?"

"The way she was chucking those snowballs at you. I also watched her technique. She rubbed the snowball, almost creating a layer of ice on it before she threw it."

"Those were hers?" he asked in shock. "The little stinker! I thought those were Dakota's."

"Nope. You're little snitch is more resourceful than you give her credit for. She may be quiet, but I have a feeling all those years by herself made her stronger than you realize."

"That kinda makes me nervous."

"Don't be. She's got a good head on her shoulders, too."

"Claire doesn't think so."

"That's because Claire still likes you."

"Then why did she break up with me?"

"Because the playboy found God and she didn't like the changes," Todd hinted as he nudged him. "You know you could get just about any girl in that building in a blink of an eye. Why aren't you dating?"

"Because I'm looking for substance, not just at the exterior. I want a Christian woman, who is strong, yet delicate. I want her to be brave, yet willing to step aside when she needs to so I can protect her. I want a girl who is good on her feet, quick witted, and observant, yet peaceful, friendly, and loyal."

"Hmmm," Todd said, thinking through his list. After a moment, he asked, "Is there an age requirement on that?"

"What do you mean?"

"You just described Miss MacKenna over there."

"Y'all were talking about me?" Katie asked, catching the last sentence Todd said. They were talking so quietly, she almost missed that one.

"No worries." Nick shook his head. "We were just talkin'."

"Loved your announcing. Thank you. It added an element of humor," Katie said gratefully.

"My pleasure. I still have to work tonight, so I didn't want to get wet anyway. You three, on the other hand, had better go get warm," Todd said, seeing Katie shivering as she stood there with her lips purple from the cold. "Sooner rather than later, eh?" He shoved Nick toward her. "You need to take better care of your charge."

"Got it," Nick said, resting his hand on the small of her back. Dakota and Todd said their good-byes as they headed down to the gate house, while Katie and Nick went to her dorm.

"Wanna see it again?" Nick asked, standing in front of the glass doors to the building.

"Yeah. Don't think I could do it right now if I tried," she said, clutching the thermos, sketchpad, and pencils in her hands for dear life. As cold as she was, she was afraid she would drop them in the snow and her sketchpad was too valuable for that.

Within seconds the door was open and they headed up the stairs. "You're really shivering," Nick said, hearing her teeth chattering.

"I-I'm c-c-cold," she stammered.

"Tell ya what," he unlocked her apartment door, "go grab a gym bag of clothes and let's go out."

"I'm f-f-freezing," she objected.

"Trust me."

"All right," she relented. Packing her clothing, towels, and toiletries into the bag wasn't easy. She couldn't feel her extremities. When she walked out to the kitchen, she asked, "Where are we going."

"Do you trust me?"

"As long as it's warm, I'll trust you."

"Not only is it warm, but you can get some exercise too."

"All right. Just a second," she said and ran to her bedroom for her sneakers, a pair of shorts, and a t-shirt to exercise in. She had already packed a pair of jeans, underclothes, and a sweater. "Okay. I'm ready."

He carried her gym bag for her to the car. On their way down, he locked the doors behind them. He wasn't sure she would be able to, as cold as she was.

It took a few minutes for the heat to kick on in his SUV and for the seats to warm up. She wasn't sure where they were going, but she didn't care either. She was starting to feel her fingers, toes, and face, and that was all she cared about at the moment.

It took them a good twenty minutes before he pulled into a parking garage. Using his key card to get into the lot, he waved at the attendant as they went through. "It's a singles building, but it's one of the more secure apartment buildings in the area. It also has a track and gym in the basement," he said as they went up the elevator from the garage.

"Yeah. Uh-huh. And the gorgeous women have nothing to do with it?"

He laughed. "You're not cutting me any slack, are you?"

"Nope. I call 'em as I see 'em."

"I know. I appreciate that. It keeps me on my toes."

Exiting the elevator, they walked down the hall to one of the apartments. "Nick! How wonderful to see you. Merry Christmas, handsome," a tall, thin, gorgeous woman gushed all over Nick from the apartment across from his. "I was hoping to see you today."

"Hey, Crystal," he cringed, "Merry Christmas to you, too."

He got the door open, but she wasn't letting him go just yet. "So, what are you doing later?" she asked, maneuvering her way between him and the door, running her fingers over the collar of his coat, flowing down from his shoulder.

Katie cleared her throat. Relief written all over his face, Nick introduced her to Crystal. "Crystal, this is Katie."

"Nice to meet you, sweetie," she said, shaking Katie's hand.

"Nice to meet you, too."

"How cute. Is she your sister?" Crystal asked.

"She's my girlfriend. And, she doesn't appreciate your talking down to her," Nick said, sternly, "and neither do I."

Katie's eyes popped open for a brief moment before she decided to play along. Obviously this woman bugged Nick. She would do him the favor of getting her off his back. She crossed her arms and glared at Crystal. "No. I don't. I also don't appreciate you accosting him or molesting him either."

"Oh. Well. Sorry," Crystal apologized. "I didn't realize he was spoken for."

Katie moved between Crystal and Nick. "He is. And I would appreciate it if you wouldn't harass him anymore," she said, as Nick took the open door and slid into the apartment.

"Have a Merry Christmas," Nick said and pulled Katie into the apartment, closing the door behind them. "Whew! Thank you. She needs a leash. I swear that woman has radar on my apartment or something."

Katie waved him off. "She won't bother you again."

"Thank you. So, do you want to warm up in the shower first?"

"Sure. What are you fixin' to do?"

He smiled, with a twinkle in his eyes. "I'm going to start Christmas dinner."

Suddenly noticing the Christmas decorations around his apartment, she remembered it was Christmas. "Did you bring me over here for Christmas dinner?"

"Of course. I couldn't let you spend it alone. That's just wrong. Now, go take a shower while I cook."

"You cook?" she asked in surprise.

"Of course. I'm single. I'd starve otherwise."

"I don't believe you."

"You'll believe it when you taste it. My Nana wasn't about to let me starve."

"Nana?" she questioned.

"She's over in the pictures on the shelf. She's in the one of Serenity Wells Station."

She went over to the pictures. "I don't see a train station."

"No. A station is the term Aussie's use for a ranch."

"I see," she said, scanning the pictures. "Oh! She looks feisty," she commented, picking up the photo of an older woman standing in front of a bunch of ranch hands in front of the main house. There was only one other woman in the photo. "Is your mom in this one too?"

"Yep." He pulled out the pans he would need for dinner before he went over to the refrigerator. "Now, go get a shower."

"Okay," she said and put it back on the shelf. "Hey, what's this?" She pointed to a wind instrument that was about four feet in length. The base color was black, and it had an ornate Aboriginal design hand painted on it.

"It's my didgeridoo."

"Do you know how to play this?"

"Are you kidding? Of course I do. My mate's ol' man taught him and I, when I spent my breaks at the station. My mate's name is Pete. He pretty much grew up on the station, and I was there as much as possible."

"So, you're a country boy at heart?"

"Clearly. The city drives me a bit looney, but it goes with the job."

"I see."

He saw the wheels turning in her mind. "What are you thinking?"

"Just investigating," she teased.

"That's my job. Now, go get a shower."

"Yes, sir," she said and grabbed her gym bag on the way to the shower.

She was impressed at how neat and clean his apartment was. He had dark-brown leather furniture in the living room, as well as cedar end and coffee tables. His sixty-inch television didn't escape her eyes either. The apartment was masculine in style, but comfortable at the same time. It had a definite touch of his Australian heritage, even in the massive bathroom. The tiles were a stark white, and he had a small potted plant on the white counter and cupboards, along with a black shower curtain, and black and white photos of Australian nature and wildlife. His black and white towels added to the simplicity of the bathroom.

She turned on the water and climbed into the shower. The water was almost too hot when it hit her hands, feet, and face, but it was warm on the rest of her body. Enjoying a long shower, she waited until she could feel all of her body parts before she got out.

She decided to put on her jeans and sweater outfit until it was time to go down to the weight room. She half wondered how long he was going to kidnap her for as she put her hair into a French braid.

"You look better," he remarked when she came out of the bathroom.

Sitting on a stool at the breakfast bar, she apologized, "Sorry it was so long. I wanted to make sure I could feel all of my fingers and toes before I got out."

He shrugged her off. "No worries."

"Need a hand?"

"And have you say you helped? Nope. You just sit there and look pretty."

Katie clicked her tongue and narrowed her eyes at him.

Feeling the temperature shift in the room, Nick looked over his shoulder to see her glaring at him. "What?"

"Just sit there and look pretty? That's a disrespectful and ignorant statement."

"Sorry. That's more out of jest than anything."

"So, you're saying I'm not pretty?" she challenged, knowing exactly what he meant.

"No, I…oh boy." He hung his head. "I'm in major trouble, aren't I?"

"You can still redeem yourself."

"Really?"

"Yes. Despite the rumors, I'm not an Ice Queen yet. You can thaw the room if you use your words right," she hinted.

He leaned on the breakfast bar across from her and said, "I apologize for the derogatory insinuation. That was not my intention. I was joking about you just sitting there, not about being pretty. You are pretty, but you have the brains and wits to match…which, in my case, seems to be hazardous to my health."

"There ya go," Katie giggled, tickled by the last statement in particular.

"Did I bail myself out?"

"This time."

"Obviously I need to stay on my toes around you," he said with a smile, his dimples in full view. He then turned back to the stove to continue cooking.

"What are we having for dinner?"

"Have to wait and see."

"It's not going to poison me, is it?" she asked, as she wandered about the room looking at the pictures, videos, CDs, and books he had in various places around the room. "By the looks of things, you would think you're Mr. Laidback."

"I'm not?" he asked, surprised by her statement.

"You are, but I see you more as the playboy type."

"I was," he admitted, "until I found God. After that, a lot of things changed. I readjusted my priorities."

"Ya know, I find it odd that you don't have a girlfriend. Meanwhile, Crystal found it odd that you possibly *did* have one. What gives?"

"I haven't had a girlfriend for at least two years."

"Really? How'd you do that?" she asked, stunned.

"I told you, my priorities changed."

"Meaning?"

"My life style is not really conducive to a relationship at the moment. I make it to church as often as possible. Other than that, I'm working or going out with co-workers."

"No room for a woman?"

"If I find the right lady, I'll make room," he conceded.

"I see," she said, sitting back down on the stool.

"Why are you studying me?"

"Just research."

"For what reason?"

"Well, you seem to know an awful lot about me. I thought it only fair to find out who you are."

"At this point, I'm not even one hundred percent sure who I am, myself. I'm still learning."

"Learning?"

"Christianity is new to me. I've only been at it for a couple of years."

"And, what do you think about it?"

"I'm not sure how I've functioned this long without Him. It almost seems too easy."

"What does?"

"Giving up control of my life and giving it to the Lord. I worry less and pray often. Things don't bother me as much anymore now that I know God has it covered."

"So, you trust Him?"

"Of course. Don't you?"

Not sure how to answer him, she admitted, "Still working on that."

"What's holding you back?"

She hesitated in answering him truthfully, but changed her mind when she remembered the challenge she made to God. In order to be fair, she felt the need to explain and see where the conversation went. "It seems when anyone gets close to me, they die."

"And, you think you have something to do with that?"

"No. I'm trying to figure out why a God of love would continuously take away the people I love, starting when I was only seven years old."

He nodded in understanding, while he said a prayer to the Lord in his head for clarity of thought and mind. Navigating this conversation would be tricky and he knew the answers needed to come from The Spirit and not him. "He didn't take them away."

"He didn't stop them from dying either."

"That's a twisted way to look at it."

She sat back in her seat with her arms crossed. "Then, by all means, iron it out for me."

"Well, your mother got leukemia, but God didn't give it to her. Cancer is a product of the sin that entered the world through Adam and Eve's decisions. As far as Jax," he noticed her cringe when he said his name, but pushed forward, "he and Anna died in a fluke car accident. A tire blew. No one took them from you, it was an accident. Now, Jillian, that's a different story." He turned to face her as he promised, "I give you my word, as an agent and a gentleman, that we *will* find out who took her from the world. She was a gem that was taken too early. Again, though, that was part of the sin that entered the world."

As Katie watched him, she felt his words, but her heart was cold.

Noting the lack of response, he continued, "In Psalm 9:10, it says, 'Those who know Your name will trust in You, for You, Lord, have never forsaken those who seek You.'"

Katie gasped.

"What's wrong?"

"That was the verse that went through my mind when I made the challenge to God."

"You challenged God?" he asked, in shock. "And you call *me* arrogant. Wow." He let out a low whistle.

"What made you use that verse?"

"The Holy Spirit. I have been praying on what to say to you, and He put that verse on my heart. Have to say, though, it was very appropriate." He studied her for a moment before he asked, "Did you really challenge Him? The Lord God Almighty?"

"Yes," she admitted. "I told Him He had until the end of the winter break to prove to me He was real."

"That's brazen."

"Stop saying that," Katie said, upset. "I wanted Him to prove I could trust Him."

"And, have you reached a verdict yet?"

"No."

"Really?" he asked in amazement. "I just – I feel really bad for you."

"What? Why?"

"Because it was the easiest and best decision I have ever made. He has never let me down since. You have Him right there, knocking on your door – practically pounding. You have your head so far up your behind, though, you can't see Him standing there begging for you to follow Him. He only wants the best for you, but you keep shoving Him away. The verse says, 'Those who know Your name will trust in You, for You, Lord, have never forsaken those who seek You.' Trust Him. He has never forsaken you. He never has…and He never will. He even sacrificed His one and only Son for you to cover the payment for your sin. What else does He need to do?"

"I need to think about it."

"Right oh," he sighed, and then went back to cooking, shaking his head in bewilderment.

While he cooked, Katie absentmindedly traced the pattern on the granite countertop of the breakfast bar with her finger. *Could she really trust God?* She asked Him to prove He was real. "What would I need to do?" she finally asked, several minutes later.

"With what?"

"I asked God to prove to me He was real. He used you and a couple of other people to show me He is. If I want to follow Christ, and trust God to lead me to whatever plan He has for me, and if I want the Spirit to guide and direct my steps, what do I need to do?"

"Well, in John 3:16 and 17, it says, 'For God so loved the world that He gave His one and only Son, that whoever believes in Him shall not perish but have eternal life. For God did not send His Son into the world to condemn the world, but to save the world through Him.' The only way to get to the Father is through the Son. What do you know about Jesus?"

"I know He came down from Heaven to die on the cross for my sins. I know He was crucified on the cross, with a horrific death, in order to shed blood and atone for the sins of the world. I also know He not only died on the cross that day, but also beat death and rose again three days later. He came, giving us practical advice through the parables, as well as showed us His love for us through His sacrifice. He then went to Heaven on a cloud, but left us with the Spirit for guidance."

"Seriously? You know all of that and still choose to resist Him?"

"Because He keeps taking people away!" Katie said in her defense. "How am I supposed to trust a God who does that?"

In a quieter voice, he took her hands into his and said, "Because He blesses you with more people who also love you. He wants to give you everything, but He needs you to love and trust Him and Him only. You can't put faith in yourself. You can't put it in me either. I may let you down, not intentionally of course, but it may happen. God will never leave you, though. All you have to do is trust Him and follow Him."

"It seems too easy."

"He doesn't want to make it hard to follow Him. He wants to prove to you how easy life can be. Actually, let me correct that. Life won't be any easier, you will just have a safe place to go to find peace when the storms of life come roaring past."

She processed his words for a few moments before she asked, "Do you ever get scared?"

"All the time."

"How do you fight that?"

"I don't. I give it to God. He allows me to feel peace, even though I am terrified out of my mind."

"I want that."

"Ya know, for someone as intelligent as you are, I find it ridiculous that you haven't accepted Jesus as your Savior before now."

"And I find your audacity appalling."

"And I find your feistiness attractive."

"And I –" she stopped mid-sentence, realizing what he said. "I don't…" her voice trailed off, as she looked away and tucked a portion of her hair that fell out of the braid behind her ear.

"You don't have to say anything. There are characteristics in women that I find attractive," he pointed out as she turned back to him. "Look, Matthew 7:7 says, 'Ask and it will be given to you; seek and you will find; knock and the door will be opened to you.' All you have to do is ask. He's been waiting to open the door for you, but you are too stubborn to see it."

"I-I know," she reluctantly admitted.

"Then?"

"I need to think about it."

"I wouldn't think on it too long. You already seem to be on borrowed time."

"I know."

"Sometimes you can be really stubborn. I'm not going to push you, but you may need to think about your eternal security a little bit more. You challenged the Lord Almighty, and He seems to have answered your prayer, but you're still resisting. You may want to rethink your position."

"I'll think about it."

"That's all I ask. Now, back to dinner," he said with a smile.

*   *   *

Dinner, to Katie's surprise was scrumptious! She didn't want to admit it, but he *was* a good cook. His grandmother taught him well. The turkey breast was plump and juicy. The

107

fresh salad was crisp, and the mashed potatoes and homemade gravy were well-paired with the steamed asparagus. The only thing that topped it was the apple pie and ice cream. He confessed to her, though, that the apple pie was store bought.

Down in the gym area, while she speed walked on the treadmill, he worked with weights.

"This is a nice building. I really like that the gym and track are down here too," Katie said, and then took a drink from her water bottle. Nick was several feet from her, bench-pressing what Katie calculated to be around two hundred and fifty pounds. "Ya know, you could probably bench-press me," Katie pointed out. "How much is that? Two-fifty?"

"Three hundred," he corrected. "The bar weighs fifty pounds. You can't be more than one-thirty, though. I could shot put you," he teased.

"I'm one-fifty," she admitted. "I'm tall. I hide it well."

He chuckled. "You could probably stand to gain a few pounds."

"How much do you weigh?"

"About two-fifty."

"I would have never guessed. You're pure muscle."

"That's the point. Muscle mass weighs more than fat."

"Yep, you don't have an ounce of that," Katie said under her breath.

"What was that?" he asked. "I didn't hear you."

"Nothing," she said quickly. After a moment, she asked, "Why don't you go out with another agent?"

"Well," he placed the barbells on the rack and sat up, "first off, you're not allowed to date within your unit." He wiped his face with a towel before taking a swig of water. "Secondly, as I said, my life won't allot for that at the moment."

"But, wouldn't another agent have the same constraints? I would think you would have women falling all over you."

He took a sip just before she said her last sentence. When she did, he spit it out and broke out in a coughing fit. Collecting himself, he wiped his face off and cleared his throat. "I'm sorry, what was that?"

"I *said* I would think you would have women falling all over you," she reiterated, turning the treadmill off. "You're a good looking guy. I'm sure there are good looking girls in that agency of yours."

"There are," he said, cautiously.

"Then, why don't you date from around your office building? They would already have clearance."

"They do."

"Then?" She gestured for him to go on.

"While there are women I'm attracted to, I don't want them to like me just for my looks. I'm not that shallow."

"So, are you saying you could snap your fingers and get a date like that?" she asked, snapping her fingers for effect.

"I'm saying I want a woman who is a thinker. I want a woman who is level-headed. I also want a woman with a great sense of humor and who can stand up for herself. But, and this is the most important, I want a woman who is a Christian. Now," he held his hand up to stop her from opening her mouth, "if she happens to be pretty, that's a bonus. What's inside her will outshine whatever is on the outside."

Stunned by the depth of his sincerity, she commented, "Wow. Okay, that was impressive. There's hope for you yet."

He burst out in laughter. "Nice. And, here, I thought we were making progress in our friendship."

"We are. I wouldn't tease you if I didn't like you."

"I see."

"Don't worry about it, though. I only get those zingers in to keep you on your toes."

"That you do very well."

"Sometimes a little too well," she admitted.

"Hence your nickname the Ice Queen?"

"Exactly. They use other terms too, but I would rather not get into those."

He crossed his arms, studying her for a moment. "Why aren't *you* dating? I'm sure there are plenty of guys who want to date you."

"Oh, there are. Ethan and Seb are on the top of that list, and don't make that a secret at all. I've also had other guys ask me out, but I turned them down as well."

"Why?"

"For a couple of reasons. One of them is because I want to keep myself pure, and guys in college only seem to have one thing on their mind."

"Wait a minute."

"What?"

He gave her a confused look as he asked, "Didn't you just have Giovanni Rossi in your apartment last night?"

"Yes."

"For two and half hours?"

"Yes," she said, wondering where he was going with the conversation. "What's your point?"

"And you're telling me you didn't do anything?"

"What do you mean? We ate dinner and played Texas Hold 'em."

"You play Texas Hold 'em?"

"I'm from Oklahoma. Of course I do."

"Hold onto that thought, go back to the Giovanni thing."

Crossing her arms in agitation, she asked, "What does Giovanni have to do with this conversation?"

"Are you telling me you're not attracted to him?"

"I can't be. He's my assignment and I'm his friend."

"How do you compartmentalize that?"

"How do you?"

"What do you mean?"

"I'm sure they have you use your looks to get information. We've already covered that area."

"True."

"Well, I would imagine you can pretend to be attracted to the woman without really being attracted to her, right?"

"Right."

"How do you keep them straight? How do you shut off your feelings while pretending to have the hots for the woman? Has that line ever been crossed?"

"No."

"Why not?"

"Because of my past. I flirt, but I don't give them my heart. The only woman I will give my heart to is my wife."

"Okay. So, if you can do that, why can't I?"

"Because you're twenty. You're hormonal," he said. As soon as he said it, he regretted it. Anger shot through her face and he momentarily saw her hazel eyes flash green and her body stiffened.

"I'm *what*? Where do you get off saying something like that?" she demanded.

"Oh boy. I did it again, didn't I?"

Narrowing her eyes at him, she didn't otherwise move a muscle.

"You look madder than a cut snake!"

"I guess that's what makes you a good agent," she said, sarcasm dripping all over her words, "your powers of observation are impeccable."

He dropped his head, shaking it. He looked back up at her and asked, "Are we going to make it through this assignment alive?"

"Only if you learn to choose your words carefully. Speaking of which, you want a shovel to unbury yourself?"

"Yes. Please?"

"You have one shot. You'd better make it good. I don't like you as it is."

He chuckled.

"Not a good start."

He got up from the bench and walked over to where she stepped down from the treadmill. Standing in front of her, he took her hands into his and admitted, "I put my foot in my mouth again. I didn't mean hormonal in the way that some men say women get every month. I meant that it's normal at your age to be a bit boy crazy."

"I have *never* been boy crazy."

"I know. I shouldn't have said it. I'm sorry."

"Yes, you are sorry."

"Hey," he said with a smile, "I'm trying to apologize, but you keep cutting into me. How can I say I'm sorry so you'll forgive me?"

"You still haven't asked that."

"Oh," he nodded in understanding, "will you forgive me for insulting you?"

"Yes."

"And, will you help me keep my size twelves out of my mouth?"

"I will," she conceded. "And, you're forgiven."

"Good. I don't think I would be able to sleep knowing you were that mad at me," he said, going back over to the bench for his towel.

"Why not?"

"Because you're a good kid. I don't like to see you angry."

"You have a funny way of showing it. You keep insulting me left and right. Speaking of which, *good kid*? I'm a *young lady*. Just when you were starting to dig yourself out of the hole, you jump right back into it again."

He nervously cleared his throat, knowing she was right. "Let me rephrase that. I don't like to see you angry, but for some reason I keep slipping up in front of you."

Leaning on the treadmill, she asked, "Yeah. Why is that?"

"Trust me," he sighed, "I wish I knew."

"Well, time will tell."

"Speaking of time. I should probably get you back to your dorm," he said, glancing at the clock in the weight room. "Do you want another shower before you go?"

"That would be appreciated. I would hate to sweat all over your truck."

"No worries. Let's go," he said, and they headed back up to his apartment.

*   *   *

Katie took a shower first, and while she packed her gym bag in the living room, Nick took his shower.

"You want to watch a movie or go back to your dorm?" Nick asked, coming out of the bathroom fully dressed about ten minutes after he went in.

"Um, I should probably get back. I've taken enough of your day."

"Oh! Wait!" He ran over to his Christmas tree and pulled a present from under it, which was about fourteen inches long, seven inches wide, and only three inches tall. "Here you go. Merry Christmas," he said, handing it to her.

"What's this?"

"It's Christmas. It's a present. Traditionally, people give presents to other people on Christmas," he said, tongue in cheek.

"Thank you. I'm afraid I didn't get you anything, though."

"You don't have to. For me, it's the giving, not the getting."

"I'm afraid I'm not used to getting something without giving something in return."

"Open it already," he encouraged.

She gasped when she opened it. "Oh my!" It was a deluxe sketch box which contained everything she would need in an all-inclusive drawing kit. "I've never gotten anything even remotely close to this!" she said in shock, running her fingers tenderly over the metal case with the photo of its contents.

"Your drawings are incredible. While you have some of those tools, this puts it all in a kit for you. You can make them even better than they already are. Also," he ran into his bedroom and returned with a larger sketch pad for her, "I didn't want to wrap this. Look, I know drawing is relaxing for you. I realize in the FBI asking you to do what we did, it has added stress to your life that wasn't there before and I wanted to let you know, as your handler, I'm there for you whenever you need me."

"I…thank you," she said and gave him a hug. "This is one of the best presents I've ever gotten."

When she looked up at him, he had to contain his emotions that suddenly wanted to take over. *Could he really be falling for a woman seven years younger than him?* "My pleasure. To see the happiness in your face gives me tremendous joy. That's the only Christmas present I need. My entire family is in Australia and Montana, so all I have are my co-workers. You gave me an excuse to give more than just cards this year."

Taking a step back, and with a grateful heart she said, "I understand that more than you know."

"Oh, I know you do."

"I'll tell you what. Why don't we start over? I think with today's conversations that I have seen you in a different light."

"Even though I put my foot in my mouth multiple times?"

"To be honest, I kind of set you up on those."

"Really?"

"Yeah. I don't like that you're arrogant and egotistical. When I find someone like that, it's my natural reaction to humble them."

"Oh, you humble me all right. I am still hearing about it from my co-workers."

"Sorry about that."

"No worries." He waved her off. "I don't mind. It brings laughter to a job that isn't the easiest. Working in an Organized Crime Unit, you see stuff that makes you wonder about humanity. Joking around helps us cut lose."

"Twisted, but it works, I guess."

"It does. C'mon, let's get you to your dorm." He ushered her down to his SUV. "I don't want to catch it tomorrow from

Todd as to why I had you out all night. Nor do I want the insinuations. You are pure and I want to keep your reputation that way too."

"Thank you," she beamed in pleasure. "See, you *can* be a gentleman when you want to."

"I can when I want to. I can be a turkey when I want to as well."

"Why doesn't that surprise me?"

"Because you figured me out faster than most. Keep those good powers of observation. They will serve you well in this business."

* * *

Aaron showed up at her dorm around ten o'clock that night. "We have got to stop meeting like this," Katie smiled, opening the door.

"It's Christmas," he said, dressed in a Santa suit.

Katie smirked, catching sight of his bike. "So, Santa's new sleigh is a motorcycle?"

"Just dropping off a little Christmas cheer. I finished at the children's wing in the hospital around nine, and drove around for a bit. Then I got a bright idea."

"What was that?"

"Well, I checked my *naughty and nice list* and realized I forgot to give you your present."

"Really?" she asked, amused, as she leaned against the doorway. "Am I naughty or nice?"

"Well," he nervously cleared his throat as he blushed, "it seems that it depends on who you talk to."

"Well, don't you see and hear everything? Aren't you Santa?"

"Well, I have elves who help out a lot in that area."

"And, according to the elves, was I naughty or nice?"

"Seems you've been very nice."

"Good. The check must have cleared that I wrote to them."

He chuckled as he pulled a present out of his red velvet bag. "I have one present left. It's for you," he said, handing her a small package.

She opened it to find a multi-colored striped scarf, with a hat to match. "I love it!" she exclaimed, putting them on.

He nodded in approval. "You look cute. Perfect colors."

She gave him a hug as she said, "I promise. While it stinks now, things *will* get better with time."

He held her a little longer than he should have before he took a step back. "I don't know about that."

"No one can ever take her place. There will always be a hole in your heart. Trust me, I know what I'm talking about. But, know that someday God will place someone in your life that will make your head spin."

"Said the one who has shut every eligible bachelor down on campus who has had an interest in her. How about taking a little advice from Santa?"

"What's your advice?"

"It's okay to be a little naughty once and awhile. You have yourself so in control, you aren't alive and free."

"I'll take that into consideration."

"Lighten up and be free. You're a prisoner of your past, Katie. I haven't seen you smile in weeks."

"I'll consider it."

He clicked his tongue as he rested his hand on the side of her face. "You're like a sister to me. I hate to see you so sad…so protective of yourself." Crossing his arms, he leaned on the other side of the doorway. "You need to be more free."

"But, not too free," she corrected him.

"Free enough to experience life, and live it to the fullest. That's what I want for you."

"That's what I want for you too," she said, giving him another hug. "Merry Christmas, Aaron."

"That's Santa," he chuckled. "And, Merry Christmas to you, Katie."

Chapter 5

Navigating the Storm

The next morning, she grabbed her breakfast and headed down to the game room to watch the news while she ate. After only a few minutes of watching, she shut the television off and went back upstairs. When she watched the news, all she got was a feeling of chaos and anger. The world was a place slowly dying, and she could feel it. She decided in feeling it, that she needed to see beauty so she bundled up and headed outside with her new sketch kit and her old sketch pad, saving the new one for after the old one was filled.

*   *   *

Dakota got the call before she left the dorm that she was going to take a walk and do some drawing. He, in turn, contacted Nick, who said they were having a meeting and he would be there after they let out. He also told Dakota he would fill him in on the meeting when he got there.

*   *   *

"So, what do we have?" Seth asked, walking into the office that morning with a cup of coffee in hand.

"Here are the six girls who were attacked and raped," Claire put their photos up on the dry erase board along the bottom. "And, here is Director Shaw's daughter, who was not only attacked, but killed as well."

"Okay, what else do we have? Emma? What do you have for a profile or MO?"

"Well, in looking at the girls there is an obvious connection in looks," Emma pointed out. "They are all around the same height, have long, black hair, and a build that is reasonably the same as well."

"Ya know, they kind of look like Katie. Can we possibly use that to our advantage?" Todd asked.

"Abso-*bloody*-lutely *not*!" Nick said adamantly.

"Why not?"

"For one, she's doing another job for us. For another, I don't want to put her in that position."

"Why not? Doesn't she want to work for the FBI?"

"She does," Seth jumped into the conversation, "but, I have to agree with Nick on this. We need her help to take the Rossi Family down. We can't do that if we're using her for bait." Turning his attention back to Emma, he asked, "What about an MO?"

"Well," she walked over to the dry erase board, "he's familiar with the campus."

"How do you know?"

"Because the areas in which these girls were attacked, were well within the boundaries of the campus. He would have to be a familiar face in order to slip in and out unnoticed. Also, the places these girls were attacked were obscure. He watched them and learned their life patterns."

"Well, that's only about twelve thousand students on an eighty-five acre campus." Todd sarcastically added, "This should be a piece of cake."

"I didn't say it was a student," Emma clarified.

"What do you mean?" Seth asked.

"I mean the male perpetrator is familiar with the campus. There are many businesses around the campus the students frequent."

Claire sighed. "This will be like finding a needle in a haystack."

"But it will be a needle we *have* to find." Director Shaw walked into the office. "There are a lot of young girls on that campus we need to protect. Jillian would search until she ran out of options if this happened to Katie. We're not going to do any less. Turn over every rock. Shake every tree. Somebody knows *something* on that campus. I have a hard time believing seven girls were attacked over a two and half year time span and no one knows anything."

"There's one more thing," Emma spoke up. Director Shaw nodded for her to go on. "The attacks happened near the beginning of a break...*all* of them. If he follows the pattern, the next one will be prior to Spring Break."

"So, we have about three months to find this cretin, and I want him found," Director Shaw said, walking back to the door. Stopping at the doorway, facing Seth's team, he added, "I won't take no for an answer on this one."

"Understood, sir," Seth acknowledged. "We'll pursue him as if Jillian was our own daughter."

"I appreciate that," Director Shaw said, and left.

When he was out of earshot, Seth added, "And I mean it. Check with every snitch you have."

"We'll find this drongo if it's the last thing we do," Nick assured him. "I don't want Katie's picture up there with the rest of those girls. Find him for these girls, Director Shaw, and for protecting one of our own, Katie."

"Whether you like it or not, she's a part of this team for now," Seth agreed, "and, due to her looks, she's a target."

"She has multiple targets on her," Todd pointed out. "We had better have a pair of eyes on her twenty-four/seven if she's going to make it to graduation."

"She *will* make it to graduation," Nick said, sternly. "I promise you."

* * *

Later that night, Giovanni picked Katie up at the dorm for dinner. "It seemed too cold to me for you to walk," Giovanni explained as they walked toward the café from the parking lot.

"I appreciate it. While I have been here for a couple of years, driving on the snow and ice still throws me a bit," she admitted, wrapping the scarf around her neck that Aaron gave her the previous night before pulling the hat down over her ears.

"So, for at least the break, would you like me to pick you up for dinner?"

"You're welcome to pick me up, but if Seb wants to walk me home, he has the first consideration."

"Are you sure you want to do that?"

"Yeah. Why?"

"Because he looks pretty ticked," Giovanni pointed out as he opened the door and saw the look on Seb's face, while he stood behind the counter with his arms crossed. "I'll tell you what. I'm pretty sure he's going to give you an earful, so I'll give you the option. Do you want me to sit with you or at the counter?"

"Why don't you start off at the counter and come over when I get things sorted with Seb. By the look on his face, it's not going to be pretty."

"I'll only let him go so far," Giovanni warned. "I'm protective when I get a friend, and I won't let him be disrespectful."

"Duly noted. And, thank you," she said appreciatively. While she headed over to their booth, he sat down at the counter.

After Seb took Giovanni's order, he headed over to Katie and sat down, opposite her in the booth. "Okay," he started, "I'm going to try to say this as nicely as possible without losing my temper."

"Okay," Katie said, uneasy.

"Have you lost your mind?"

Katie couldn't help the giggle that escaped her mouth.

"Seriously? You had mafia boy over to your apartment in a nearly empty dorm only weeks after losing Jillian? Have you lost your mind?"

"No. And, Giovanni had absolutely nothing to do with Jillian's death."

"How do you know?"

"Because he was in the library when she was killed."

"And you know that *how*?"

"Because I was in there too."

He took a deep breath to keep his emotions under control. "And, were you there *together*?"

"No. Jillian took care of that before she left."

"And, you didn't take that as a clue to listen to her? You just decided to go ahead and friend the mafia despite her warnings?"

"I'm not trying to upset anyone here."

"I'm afraid you're doing that all too well," Seb grumbled. "You set Ethan off so badly, it took me three hours to get him calmed down. Speaking of which, when he tried to call you on Christmas you weren't there. Where were you?"

"With a friend."

"You spent Christmas with mafia boy?" Seb yelled.

"No. She didn't," Giovanni said from the counter.

"Butt out. This isn't your conversation," Seb snapped.

Giovanni got up from the counter and sat in the booth next to Katie. "I know you guys call me mafia boy and I *do* believe you said, 'you spent Christmas with mafia boy,' which means you pulled me into the conversation. Also, I informed her I would not tolerate you disrespecting her, and yelling at her *is* disrespecting her. Having said that, I will return to the counter if you change the tone in which you are speaking with her."

"I-okay," Seb said, stunned by his politeness and directness. "I'm sorry for yelling at you," he apologized.

"Now, for the record, she did not spend it with me. I spent it with my family. Carry on," he said, and returned to his seat at the counter without another word.

"Wow," Seb said in shock.

"What?" Katie asked, the anger still evident on her face from him yelling at her.

"That was very nice of him."

"I *told* you he was nice, but you were too busy listening to the gossip around you to see that. He's very much a gentleman. And before you say it, *nothing* happened between us on Christmas Eve. All we did was eat and play Texas Hold 'em." Katie sat up in her seat. Feeling propelled by adrenaline, she continued, "All you guys have done over the last few weeks was call me naïve, a child, and tried to boss me around. I am *no one's* property. I am a strong young lady who reads people at their heart, not judges them by what people are saying around me. Giovanni has a tremendous heart and is more of a gentleman than I have seen anyone on this campus even come close to. And, y'all have the audacity to tell me how bad he is without even trying to be his friend or see what he's about."

With anger taking over, she yelled, "I *am not* a child. I *am not* naïve. I *will* be friends with whomever I deem an honorable, fair, and a just human being…and Giovanni is *very much* in that category, so I suggest you take *that* to the group and let them stew on it over the next two weeks. They need to make a decision to accept me for who I am and not try to control me. They need to decide if they will accept my other friendships that don't happen to be from the group. I have *never* let *anyone* tell me who to be friends with and who not to be friends with, and I *am not* about to start now."

Outside of Dominic cooking in the kitchen, not a sound was heard in the nearly empty restaurant. Not even a peep from the other family eating in the diner. All of them, children and adults, were staring at the scene in front of them with interest.

"You have a choice to make," Katie finished in a less angry tone.

Seb debated in his head for several long moments before he got up from the booth. Katie feared she lost her friend until he went over to Giovanni and stuck his hand out, and said, "I'm sorry. I judged you for what your family did, not for who you are. Do you forgive me?"

Giovanni shook his hand, speechless.

"Katie's right. You stood up to Ethan when he yelled at her, and to me when I disrespected her. You have proven yourself to be a better friend to her than we have been lately."

"That's not my intention. I only want a friend or two," Giovanni explained. "I know you guys are close. I've never had that."

Seb understood at that moment why Katie befriended him. "I'm sorry, man. I would like to get to know you as well, if you'll let me."

Giovanni's grin lit his face. "I would like that," he agreed.

"Good. Why don't you go sit with Katie and I'll get your dinner, which is on me tonight for being such a jerk?"

"No need, man. You need the money or you wouldn't be here. I appreciate the thought, though. Come on, let's see what she wants for dinner," he said and they went back over to the table to find Katie's eyes red, but she wasn't crying. "What's wrong?" Giovanni asked in concern.

"I'm not crying," she said quickly.

While Giovanni sat opposite her, Seb slid in beside her, and said, "I know you're angry with me and you have a right to be. I need to be a more supportive friend and less suffocating."

"That would be appreciated," she said to Seb. Then she turned to Giovanni and explained, "It just breaks my heart that you have to fight so hard to have a friend. You're a good guy. You shouldn't have to go through a battle in order to have someone to call a friend. That's just wrong."

"I agree," Giovanni said. "That's why I was so pleased you wanted to be my friend. That's also why I am so protective of my friends." He reached across and squeezed her hand.

She squeezed his hand in return before she let go. Then she hugged Seb and said, "I love you for your friendship as well."

"I know. I don't want to lose you, though. Everyone in the group is on edge and we don't want to see anything happen to you," he explained. "We're all still spinning from losing Jill."

"I know."

"I never expressed my condolences for your loss. I'm sorry," Giovanni said. "I only met her the one time, but I'm sure she was a great person."

"The best," Katie agreed, wiping the tear that finally escaped her eyes.

"I have a feeling we're going to need all the friends we can get in the next coming days. I know several students left the school for good, but when the rest return, people will still be recovering from the blow that someone was actually killed. They were on edge before, but this will be like navigating the blizzard from Christmas Eve. People won't know who to trust," Seb said, somberly.

"I'll tell you what," Giovanni proposed, "I'll trust you guys, if you trust me."

"Deal," Seb said, shaking his hand. "Of course, when the others come back they'll be suspicious at best."

"Yeah, my brother is the same way. I may bring him tomorrow night so he can meet you if you don't mind. He's suspicious by nature, but if he meets you at an informal setting, maybe he won't give me such a hard time."

"Why does your brother control who you're friends with?" Katie asked.

"He doesn't. He's a lot more like my dad than I am, though. I'm more like my mother was. Trust for me is hard, but for him it's virtually impossible. Whenever he *does* let someone in, they had better not betray him or they're in for a storm that will make that blizzard feel like a gentle breeze. He's a force to be reckoned with," he warned.

Katie gulped. She would have to breech that topic with Nick next time she saw him. If this was going to continue and she was to meet her goal of getting Giovanni out, his brother, Joey, would have to be discussed. While she wasn't afraid of Giovanni, she was terrified of Joey.

*   *   *

"Got some news," Emma said, running into the office.

"What's that? And, *please* let it be good news," Seth said, feeling the pressure of investigating the death of the Director's daughter, with not a lot of evidence to go on.

She grinned. "He's been collecting, but we missed it. Actually, *I* missed it."

"What are you going on about?" Nick asked.

"I missed it and I shouldn't have. It was so subtle, though, I totally missed it."

"Missed *what*?" Seth asked, getting impatient.

"Traditionally, repeat offenders, such as a serial rapist or killer, take something from their victims. It's like a trophy from each victim to remind him of them. Look, along with their looks, there's one more thing they have in common," she said, going over to the dry erase board. She put a photo of each of the girls attacked below their picture. The photos were taken after the attacks.

Todd, Dakota, Nick, and Seth stared at the pictures for a few minutes before Claire went over to see what she could see. She bent down to take a closer look, when she saw it. "They all have earrings on?" she asked.

"Yes." Emma grinned. "You got it. He took the trophy of an earring off the right ear of each girl when he finished. Look at their right ears. Even while some had multiple piercings, they each have one earring missing off their right ear."

"Twisted," Seth shook his head, "yet subtle."

"Small enough for him to have a piece of them, yet not big enough for us to catch it in the beginning," Emma explained.

"Good job." Seth patted her on the back. "That means when we find him, he should have all the earrings somewhere close to him, which would have the DNA of the girls."

Brenda Birch walked in with yet another young lady of about twenty-eight years old. "Hello, Agent Simmons, this is Sarah Thomas. She's going to be your new receptionist."

"Like the other one worked out so well?" He raised an eyebrow in question.

"She said you guys wanted her to do too much."

"We wanted her to do her job. We can't help it if she broke her finger nails on the keyboard. That's not our fault."

"Try to take it easy on this one. My list is running short."

"All right," Seth sighed, crossing his arms, "have a seat."

When she sat down, Brenda gave her a few papers to start with before she left. Sarah looked around nervously, not sure where to begin.

"When someone calls for us, unless it's another FBI office, we're not here," Seth instructed. "You are to tell them to leave a message and the agent will get back with them as soon as possible."

"Yes, sir," Sarah said, and dove into a stack of files about six inches thick.

"We still need to find the connection as to how he knows his victims," Nick said, feeling a twinge of nervousness. "Katie has earrings too," he pointed out. "They're studs, but she wears them."

"She *cannot* be alone until this is over," Seth said, looking directly at Nick. "I want her to make it to graduation, but the direction of this investigation isn't making me comfortable in getting her to that goal."

"She's got us on her campus," Dakota mentioned, "and her apartment and phone are bugged."

"I mean I want a pair of eyes on her at all times," Seth specified.

"How is that possible when she is in a practically empty dorm?" Claire asked. "No one comes back for at least two weeks. It will look odd if one of us goes in as a student this early. Christmas was just yesterday. The soonest someone would return, I would think, would be just after New Year's Eve."

"I don't care how you do it. She's to be a protected asset from this point forward. I know Jones and Samuels are currently on security, who's in the restaurant?"

"Tucker and Adams are in there with Tucker's family to fit in better. His wife doesn't know it's to watch Katie, though."

"I would think not. Nick, get with Claire and figure out how to make sure we have eyes on her," Seth instructed. "I have to give Director Shaw an update," he said, and left the room.

"I think I know how to do this," Nick said, sitting across from Claire at her desk.

"How?"

"I need to take a closer roll."

"Meaning?"

"Meaning Katie needs to introduce me to her friends, so it's not an issue for them to see me around campus."

"Oh, that'll go over *real* well. Hey, he's harmless. He's just an FBI agent. Oh? Giovanni, you have a problem with hanging out with the FBI? Really, Nick? How is that going to go over?"

"Let me work on it with her and I'll let you know," he said, mulling different scenarios around in his mind. "In the meantime, we may need an extra body in the dorm. Where's the nearest apartment to her that's empty?"

Claire hacked into the admissions office of the school with ease. She could hack into The Pentagon if she wanted to. Truth be told, she was recruited into the FBI for her hacking skills. When they arrested her for hacking into a bank, the initial deal they made gave her immunity in exchange for her working with them. After a bit, she found she enjoyed working with them, and it was no longer a punishment to her, but a reward.

"There's an apartment on the same floor, two doors down, but how are we going to get in there without using electric? I'm sure an extra light on in the dorm at night will raise suspicion."

"We get agents to stay in the empty apartment. At night, a female agent can sleep on the couch in the living room of *her* apartment, to be there in case anything happens. Then, during the day, the agents in the apartment can keep an eye on things down the hall. The wire taps can be set up in that apartment, too, instead of in the bread truck we have on campus. That will put agents closer in case something happens and we need to get to her quickly."

"Actually, that'll work out better," Claire agreed. "Now, what about when she's in classes or if she's out with her friends?"

"We'll work on the class part and come up with a plan a couple of days before school starts. As far as the other, let me work on that."

"Okay, I trust you. I'll take this to Director Shaw and Seth for recommendations on the female agents."

"In the meantime, I'm going to get to my charge," he said. "We have quite a bit to talk about."

"Yeah, would *love* to be a mouse in the house when you have *that* conversation," Dakota chuckled. "She pitched a fit when she found out we wired her room and tapped her phone. I can't *wait* to find out what she says when you inform her that an agent will be down the hall, as well as in her apartment at night."

"I'll handle it."

"She's strong willed," Todd warned.

"Right, but she wants to survive this. In order to do that, she's going to have to listen to me."

Both Dakota and Todd burst out in laughter. "Ohhh," Dakota shook his head, "You are *so* in for it. I believe you met your match in that young lady. She's a spitfire."

"Yeah," Todd agreed. "She's definitely one wildcat I would *not* want to tangle with. I'm glad she landed on your desk and not mine."

Chapter 6

Jack Frost

That night, after Seb walked her home, Katie was in her room doing her devotions. She picked Psalm 56 for her reading. The verses that stuck in her mind were verses three and four, which said, 'When I am afraid, I put my trust in you. In God, whose word I praise – in God I trust and am not afraid. What can mere mortals do to me?'

Conversations she had over the last few weeks floated through her mind. What she was doing *was* dangerous, but her heart was in the right place. Kneeling on the floor, with her hands folded on her bed in front of her, she prayed aloud "Father, I know I have been a bit stubborn when it comes to You over the last several years. I know I'm headed into a potentially dangerous situation, but I also know You had a hand in it. I know You placed these people in my life for a reason. Everything that has happened over the last few weeks has happened for a reason. I'm not sure why, but I trust You. I know without You, I won't make it. I want to ask for Your protection. I ask for the confidence in those verses. I want to trust in You and not be afraid. I want the confidence in You Nick has. I want –" She stopped short, feeling pressure on her chest. She caught her breath and admitted, "I'm scared, Jesus. I know You faced worse, but I'm scared. Jillian had a look of fear and terror on her face when we found her. I don't want that. I want peace. Will You please grant me the comfort and peace of knowing You're looking out for me? I know it's another challenge and I ask for patience and understanding from You as I sort this out," she prayed, and then sat there in silence, letting the Spirit soak into her inner core.

She had the feeling of pressure slowly reside, replaced by a feeling of peace and comfort. At that moment, she knew the Lord had heard her. She knew whatever the world sent to try to destroy her, that her Father wouldn't let her down, Jesus would be right beside her, walking every step of the way, and the Spirit would guide her steps and grant her peace when the storms of life hit. She knew at that moment she would never be alone.

*   *   *

To relax, Katie drew a picture of a scene from the snowball fight. Nick peeked around the tree while she, Dakota, and Todd threw the snowballs at him. She smiled while she drew it, remembering the fun and laughter that exploded when she threw the first snowball.

She cherished the bursts of laughter life threw her way and often froze those moments as snapshots in her sketch pad, along with other moments she didn't want to forget. While some of those were not so good, she was glad she drew them. Whether they were good memories or bad ones, they were memories that shaped her into who she had become.

After she got the basic picture of the snowball fight down, she went back and flipped through other moments in her drawings. Cherishing each of the memories represented in the sketches, she realized just how much she missed her friends from Oklahoma. It also dawned on her how the horrible memories represented made her stronger. The memories that were in the sketchpad included one that she drew of what she remembered from her mother's funeral, where little seven-year-old Ryan held her hand beside the grave. She also drew a picture of her father shaking her in anger while her feet dangled in the air. There was another picture of the first football game Jax played the saxophone at, where she, Emily, and Ty sat near the band. Then there was the picture she drew of the forest when she first met Serenity, followed by a picture of the Homecoming Dance with Jax. There were multiple pictures of the group going to events, including some of their weekends at the lake, dances, and attending games. Then there was the last one of Jax before the individual pictures of her friends, it was at the lake the weekend before prom.

Turning to the page after the snowball picture, she drew the car accident scene as best she could remember it. Drawing fast and furious, the pencil almost moved on its own. After she drew the basic, she centered on Officer Williams, and drew a picture of a man behind him who was glowing. Baffled and confused, she kept drawing. It only took her a few moments before she realized she was drawing Jesus. He was there. At the accident, He had His hand on the officer, keeping him calm for Katie.

Tears flowed from her eyes as she continued to draw. After she drew Ty, she drew what turned out to be an angel holding his hand while he whispered in Ty's ear. Then she drew Jax, to see the angel crying who was sitting next to him, holding his lifeless body. When she drew Anna, there was also an angel crying as she held her. She wanted to stop, but she kept drawing and found herself drawing an angel next to her as well. The angel had his hands around her head, keeping her calm. She shook her head. *How did she miss that? How did she not know Jesus was there?*

She jumped when she heard a knock on her apartment door. Quickly brushing off the tears from her face, she ran for the door in her jeans and sweater. Sliding in her socks on the linoleum flooring, she almost missed the front door.

When she looked through the peephole, she saw Nick in the hallway with a woman. Curiously, she opened the door. "Hey," she said, hoping to hide that she had been crying, knowing in the back of her mind it would be impossible to hide that she was crying from anyone who truly knew her.

"Hey," he said. He cringed before his face softened. He knew she was crying, and he would tackle that one after he talked about why the woman was there. "Katie MacKenna, this is Agent Serrin Matthews. She is one of many agents who will be staying with you through the break. In the evenings, a female agent will sleep on the couch. If you feel uncomfortable, feel free to lock your bedroom door."

Confused, she said, "I don't understand."

"Serrin, please give me a minute with her?" Nick asked.

"Sure. It'll give me time to set up in the other apartment," she said and left the two of them.

They went into the living room and sat down. Nick took a deep breath before he said, "There have been some developments, and as a valuable FBI asset, we need to make sure you're protected at all times. Now," he held his hand up to stop her from talking when she went to object, "Now, knowing you are in the apartment by yourself in a practically empty dorm and on a nearly deserted campus, we need the agent to be in this apartment at night. During the day, they will be in the abandoned apartment two doors down on the other side of the hallway. That is also where a station has been set up to monitor the bugs here in the apartment and the wiretap on your phone line."

"Okay. What kind of developments?"

"It's regarding the case of the attacker on campus. It seems along with the physical similarities of the victim's builds and looks, the attacker also took an earring from their right ear as a trophy. Now couple that with the similarities of the girls attacked strongly resembling yourself, you being on this campus practically by yourself, *and* being a friend with Giovanni Rossi, you now have multiple targets on you," he explained.

"Um, speaking of that, Giovanni wants Seb and me to meet his brother, Joey."

"Really?"

"Yes. He's fixin' to bring him tomorrow night to the café."

"And, what do you think about that?"

"I'm nervous," she admitted. "I just finished praying about it with God. I prayed out loud, forgetting you guys were listening."

"We don't listen to spy on you. We listen to come running if something happens. Something like your prayers are personal. We listen, but don't pay attention. Now, speaking of paying attention, I see by your eyes that you have been crying. Does this have anything to do with your prayer?"

"No. Stay here," she said and ran into her room. When she returned, she showed him the picture she drew of the car accident. "This is why I was crying."

He studied it a few moments before he asked, "Does this mean you now know He was with you through the whole thing?"

"Yes. And, hopefully He'll be with me until the end."

"I believe that's up to you," he hinted.

"I'm still working on that."

"What's stopping you?"

"It's a trust thing. I'm working on it."

"Whatever," he sighed. He flipped a page back in her sketchbook. Katie objected, but it was too late. "What's this?" he asked.

Her face flushed in embarrassment. "I like to freeze moments in time. Preferably happy ones," she explained.

He turned back another couple of pages to find the picture of the group at the lake house. "Is this the last picture you drew before the one you drew on the day of the snowball fight?"

She nodded. "Outside of this one," she pointed to the picture of her friends from the neck up, "If it wasn't an assignment, I didn't draw."

"Shame," he said, feeling bad for her. "For two-and-a-half years, the only things you drew were assignments?"

"Yes."

"That's really a shame. I know that's how you find your peace. You need to do it more often."

"It's hard to keep your heart ice-cold when it gets melted."

"Meaning?"

"Meaning when I draw I connect with God and He penetrates my heart. I was running from Him. I couldn't do that if I drew."

"I see. And now that you're trying to connect with Him?"

"I can draw."

He nodded in understanding.

"I just wish I could be free. I feel like I'm under a magnifying glass with everyone watching and listening to everything I say and do."

"It's for your safety and our peace of mind. You're the only one who can get into the Rossi family. You're the only one with a connection to Giovanni that is building to be strong enough to get him out."

"And, if I get killed by the attacker…" her voice trailed.

"Giovanni's stuck."

"He'll never be free," she concluded.

"Exactly. His freedom hinges on your connection. If your connection is severed, our chances of bringing down the Rossi family fall."

"And, so does Giovanni."

"It's all up to you."

"Right," she commented sarcastically, "No pressure there."

*   *   *

Aaron stopped by after his concert that night. "Hey. I know you said not to make this a habit, but I had to stop by. I had a revelation."

"Really?" Katie asked, sitting down on the couch with him in the lobby.

"Yeah. I love you, but I don't want to be like you."

"Um, what does that mean?"

"You're so shut down. You won't let anyone else into your heart. You say when you get to know them, they get taken away." Pacing in front of the couch, he organized his thoughts. "Please don't take it the wrong way, but I don't want to be shut down like you are. I want to experience life. I want to live life. I think Jillian would want me to."

"What about the anger?"

"Oh, the anger is still there. I *will* find out who killed her. And, when I do, they'll regret it. However, I don't want to lose out on love just because I lost Jillian. I'm not going to go looking for it, but I *am* going to make myself open to the opportunity."

"I see."

"Actually, I don't think you do. I'm not interested in anyone at the moment. I just think Jillian would want you open to it as well."

"Aaron," she shook her head.

"Oh, no! I don't mean me," he clarified. "I love you like a sister. And besides, you and I wouldn't make a good match."

"No," she chuckled, "we wouldn't."

"But I *do* know a couple very nice gentlemen who would be a more than suitable match for you," he hinted.

"I'll go at my pace."

"No. You're going to shut yourself down to the point that you'll never let anyone in."

Sighing, she crossed her arms. "I'll let someone in."

"Do you promise?"

She nodded. "Yes. I promise you that I will let another man in when the time is right."

"Good. For me, to see you happy and in love would be the best Christmas present ever."

"Consider it done."

"Great. Well, I need to get back home. It's cold and getting colder."

"Wait a minute," she said, running for the staircase. She came back down with the scarf and hat he gave her the previous night. "It's too cold to not have a scarf or hat."

"Thank you." He accepted them. "I'll bring them back to you tomorrow."

"I appreciate that."

As he went to leave, he asked, "Do you know if the mailroom is still open?"

"No, but there should still be access to your mailbox. Why?"

"Because I'm supposed to have a credit from the school in it and I want to make sure. It seems that the financial aid office had another grant of mine come through. That's great for me. With money in my pocket, it's a nice way to start the upcoming year, huh?"

"Definitely!"

"Well, get some sleep, huh, kiddo?" he said, giving her a hug before he left.

*   *   *

Aaron pulled open his mailbox in the mailroom of Fenn Tower to find the financial aid notice exactly where they said it would be. He started to call Katie to let her know his good news was accurate, when he heard a noise down the hall.

His heart raced as he went to investigate. Walking past the dark fitness center, he felt an arm go around his neck, cutting off his air. Adrenaline took over when he realized this was the attacker. This was the one who took his Jillian away from him!

*   *   *

As soon as the attacker heard the grunt and growl of a man's voice under his arm, panic filled him. He knew Katie wore a scarf and hat identical to the one the man was wearing the night before to the restaurant, and with the lanky body and long black hair sticking out from under it, he assumed it was Katie.

He felt the ram of an elbow into his side with such force, it cracked a couple of his ribs. Suddenly Aaron spun around and grabbed his right wrist and twisted it behind the attacker's back so fast, it stunned him as he shoved him into the wall. Using his advantage of size, the attacker rammed his foot down Aaron's calf to smash a couple of bones in his foot. When Aaron went to the ground, the attacker thrust a knife into Aaron's upper mid-section, puncturing his liver. He then used the scarf to tighten around Aaron's neck, cutting off his air supply. He had to silence this young man. He couldn't let him get away.

"You killed Jillian. Didn't you?" Aaron accused, as he struggled to get air, while flailing his arms, hitting him wherever he could. "You're a coward! You don't deserve to be alive!"

The attacker tightened the scarf as tight as he could. Aaron grabbed the scarf, leaving his bloody handprint on it as he collapsed on the floor.

"You will rot in hell…for what you did to those girls!…I may not…but someone *will* kill you. When they do…I'll cheer them on," he squeaked out.

"Then you'll do it from the grave," the attacker said as Aaron went unconscious.

When Aaron was on the ground, he slid the scarf off him and tucked it into the pocket of his hooded sweatshirt. He knew it was Katie's. He wasn't sure what Aaron was doing with it, but he felt it was his duty to get it back to her.

As he left Aaron's body behind, he stepped on Aaron's phone, crunching it beneath his boot. "Looks like I win after all."

When the attacker left the building, Aaron slowly opened his eyes. Seeing his phone shattered, he knew he couldn't use it, but he had to warn someone of who the attacker was.

He pushed up with his hands to get off the floor, but slipped on his own blood, dropping back onto the ground. Using the blood that poured from his body onto the tile flooring around him, taking his life with it, he wrote the letter 'C' before he slipped back into unconsciousness, closely followed by death.

*   *   *

Fumbling his keys with his trembling hands, the attacker opened the door to his house. He couldn't believe what he did. He killed someone…again. Running to the bathroom, he scrubbed his hands as hard as he could, watching the blood run down the drain until the water was clear.

When he finished, he went down to the basement and turned the light on. He took a deep breath as he surrounded himself with photos of Katie. "Someday, my love," he said, hanging the scarf with the bloody handprint on the wall. "Someday you will be mine and I will be yours. Then all of this will be worth it."

*   *   *

Katie had a difficult time trying to get to sleep that night. She got up in the middle of the night and peeked out into the living room to see the agent awake, playing on her phone. "You awake?" Katie asked.

Serrin set her phone aside as she sat up on the couch. "Yes, the question is why are *you* awake?"

Sitting on the chair next to the couch, Katie wrapped herself tighter in her comforter to keep warm and sighed. "I have a lot on my mind."

"Want to download some of that?"

"If you don't mind?"

"Of course. I have to stay awake anyway. We're not allowed to sleep while we're guarding you at night."

"That stinks."

"It does, but I'd rather be alert and not miss something until it's too late."

"I appreciate that."

"Now, what's on your mind?"

"Well, I'm fixin' to meet Giovanni's brother tomorrow. While Giovanni doesn't scare me, his brother does."

"Why? What's the difference between the two?"

"Giovanni's heart is in the right place. The way Giovanni has talked about his brother, though, it tells me he's a scary, calculating individual."

"Hence the reason we're here."

"And, what about the attacker?"

"That's the other reason we're here. Nick is a great agent. He protects his charges with everything in him…and for the record, that's a lot. Anyone would want him on their squad."

Katie nodded in understanding. "Okay, I'm impressed. I judged him pretty harshly."

"Actually, from what I hear, you judged him accurately. He puts that mask on for self-preservation. He doesn't want to get hurt."

"What do you mean?"

"He has a heart. He's been hurt a lot, not saying he didn't do his share, though. He's changed quite a bit over the last few years."

"He mentioned that."

"I mean he's changed *a lot*. He used to use women."

"But, he doesn't anymore?"

"Nope. As a matter of fact, he's gone the other direction."

"I see."

"I'm telling you this so you can understand him. I don't normally tell people about their handlers, but I think with what you're about to walk into, you need to trust him."

"I know."

"I mean trust him absolutely. If he tells you to duck, don't ask why. If he tells you to jump, do it and ask later."

"That scary, huh?"

"Yes. I don't want to alarm you, because you're already losing sleep, but you have to understand the reality around you.

I need you to rely on him and follow his lead. I need you to understand he knows what he's doing."

"I do. And, I trust him."

"Good. If you follow what he tells you, you'll make it through this. If you do it right, your friend won't have to lead the Rossi family either."

"Right."

"Your motives are pure. You have to separate yourself from your heart when it comes time to approach the subject of getting him to flip."

"Yeah. How do I do that?"

"You don't. Let Locke do that. He'll lead you. You have the connection. Let him instruct you on how to use it."

"I will."

"Now, before Jack Frost nips at your nose and you get too cold to sleep, go get some rest."

"You're right. Thank you for the talk."

"Anytime," she said, and went back to her phone while Katie shuffled to her room.

When Katie sat down on her bed, she opened her sketch pad to the drawing of the accident she drew earlier. Working on it until she couldn't keep her eyes open anymore, she fell asleep, pencil in hand.

Chapter 7

Let It Snow

Katie woke up the next morning to find Nick in the living room talking with Serrin. They both had a somber look on their faces. "So serious this early in the morning," Katie commented as she pulled the orange juice from the refrigerator. "That can't be good."

"Um, can you put that back in the fridge and come over here with us?" Nick asked. "We need to talk."

Remembering the conversation she and Serrin had the night before, she followed Nick's instructions and sat down next to Serrin. When Serrin took Katie's hand into hers, Katie's heart raced in panic. "What's going on?"

"Sometime around ten or ten-thirty last night, Aaron Sawyer was killed in Fenn Tower near the mailroom."

"Aaron...*what*?" Feeling like she got punched in the stomach, Katie thought sure she was going to throw up. "No. He was here at ten. You have to have your times mistaken. Maybe it's not him."

Nick pulled a plastic bag out of his pocket that contained Katie's hat, and handed it to her in an answer.

With her hands shaking, Katie took the clear plastic bag. She threw the bag to the side as she bolted for the bathroom, barely making it before she vomited. Shaking and pale, she had no idea what to do or think. She had spoken to Aaron only minutes before he was taken.

Dropping her head into her hands, she reviewed the conversation in her mind. While she made a promise to him, could she keep it knowing she could yet lose someone else in her life?

"Katie?" Serrin knocked on the door. "Katie, can I come in?"

"I don't…" She threw up again. Her nerves were raw and she had absolutely nothing in her stomach.

Serrin slowly opened the door. Resting her hand on Katie's back as she crouched next to her, she asked, "You said he was here at ten last night?"

Katie nodded in response.

"Did you give him your scarf and hat last night?"

She nodded again.

"We found a letter from the school, along with his cell phone near him."

Katie nodded again.

"Please talk to me?"

She burst into tears as her body trembled uncontrollably. "He-he was here only minutes before. Why would someone kill him? He wouldn't hurt anyone but…" Katie looked up at her, wide-eyed.

"But what?"

"The attacker. He promised to kill the attacker. That would be the only person he would hurt."

"His foot was broken, along with a couple of his fingers. Whoever attacked him, Aaron got a good piece of them too."

Katie perked up. "DNA. There should be DNA on him from the attacker."

"Sorry, no. There was something interesting, though."

"What?"

"There was a letter 'C' on the floor, written in his blood. We're pretty sure he was trying to tell us who killed him. Do you know anyone with the letter 'C' in their name?"

With her mind now kicked into gear, it swirled with ideas and thoughts, distracting her from the vomit that wanted to come up. "Just Cierra, but she's not here. Her family went to Colorado for Christmas. Besides, he wouldn't hurt Cierra, and Cierra wouldn't hurt a fly."

"I agree," Serrin said, now in thinking mode as well. Happy to have distracted Katie enough that Katie wouldn't dwell on the loss, she kept the momentum going. "Is there anyone else you can think of?"

"Not really."

Nick leaned on the doorway with his arms crossed. "We need to get some food in your stomach."

"Um, not yet."

"What can you tell us about last night?"

Serrin shook her head at Nick before she said to Katie, "Don't worry about that for now. Just focus on the letter 'C' and who it could be."

"We need –"

"To let her mind and stomach settle," Serrin said sternly, cutting Nick off. "Use some discretion here. Go make her some toast with butter, will you?"

"Am I being dismissed?" he asked, stunned.

"For the moment, yes."

"Wow. And they call me brazen," he said and left for the kitchen.

"Just let your stomach settle and keep concentrating on the letter 'C.' I have a feeling the key to this is in your mind. I have a feeling you already know who it is, only you don't realize it. Nick's getting you some toast. Just come out when you're settled."

As Katie nodded in response, Serrin went into the kitchen to find Nick standing in front of the toaster. "She was a mess, but when I got her mind working, it overrode her mourning instinct," Serrin explained.

"She shouldn't stuff it, though. She's already shut down with the loss of Jillian. She really needs to mourn them both. The only reason she's worked through the loss of Jax and Anna was due to Stacey. I'm still debating on recommending her going to Stacey's house for the remainder of break."

"If you do, you could lose the momentum of her with Giovanni."

"If I don't, I could lose her. She may just shut down permanently."

"If she's going to be an agent, that might not be a bad thing," Serrin pointed out.

"I don't want her to. Her heart makes her who she is."

"You can't dictate how she deals with things. While she is your charge, you're not in charge of her life. You're her handler."

"I feel responsible for bringing her into this."

"And in doing so, you may actually save her life. Let time sort this out. Let God sort this out. Look, you and I both know we're Christians." She glanced over her shoulder to make sure Katie wasn't listening before she turned back to Nick. "We know God works in mysterious ways. We have to let Him guide how she deals with things. We have to let the Spirit guide her and her steps."

"She's resisting, though."

"It's all in His timing."

He sighed as he crossed his arms. "Sometimes I wish His timing moved a little faster."

"His timing is not our timing, but it's *always* perfect."

"I know."

"Knowing and applying are two different things. Let Him work on her heart while you save her life."

* * *

Katie worked on her drawings all through that day, lost in thought. She sharpened the images from the snowball fight and made a new drawing of a memory she had. It was of her college friends when they were at a football game. She sighed when she drew Jillian. Jillian was in her element when she was at a sporting event, cheering.

When she drew Aaron, though, she broke out in tears. She pushed through it and finished the picture with her hands shaking. Praying the entire time that she would not lose any more friends, she steadied her hands as much as possible. With all of the loss she had experienced, she wasn't completely sure how much more she could handle.

*   *   *

Around four-thirty, the bell rang for the dorm. She knew it would be Giovanni, so she ran down the stairs to meet him. When she reached the lobby, she was stunned to see Nick standing there. "I'm sorry. I thought…you can't be here. Giovanni will be here any minute."

"I know. I need to meet your college friends and I think I may have a way to help you get rid of your Ice Queen reputation in the process."

She crossed her arms. "Oh, really? How's that going to work?"

"You need to introduce me as your boyfriend. That will get Seb, Ethan, and whoever else wants to date you off their radar. Also, you'll be protected because I can be by your side and not raise suspicions."

She nervously tucked her hair behind her ear. "I don't know about that one. It'll hurt Seb and Ethan."

"Do you or don't you want to date them?"

"Not really. I don't want to lose them as friends either, but I'm afraid if I cross that line, it will happen."

"Then, let me rescue you from all of that."

"Rescue me? I don't need rescuing. I've been treading water just fine."

"Right. But if you recall, you now have several targets on your back, and Serrin said you were worried about meeting Joey tonight. Why not surprise everyone? That would explain where you were on Christmas Day."

"The other family in the restaurant last night wasn't really a family, were they?" Katie asked, connecting a couple dots in her mind, as he referenced the conversation between her, Seb, and Giovanni in the café.

"No. Well, yes, they were a family, but the guys were FBI."

"And they were there for my dinner."

"Right. Now they won't have to be if I'm with you. What do you say? I promise that you will make it to graduation. In order to do that, with the loss of Aaron now too, I need to either have an agent by your side or in the room with you. The easiest way to do that is to pretend to be your boyfriend. Will you play along with whatever I come up with?"

"According to Serrin, I should do whatever you say. In this case you're asking permission, and I appreciate it, but it's not necessary. I think that would put you in a better position to help me flip Giovanni. I gotta ask, though. Why did you wait to talk to me about it down here and not go to the apartment?"

"Because I didn't want it on tape."

"I see."

"It's between us."

"Understood. And, yes, I'll go along with it."

"Good," he said, and pulled her toward him and kissed her.

She was so caught by surprise she almost hit him before she heard the bell for the dorm go off, meaning he saw Giovanni before she did.

When he pulled away, he whispered, "Company."

"I caught that," she said, catching her breath. She had to admit he was a fantastic kisser.

"You okay?" he asked, steadying her when she wavered a bit.

"I was just caught off guard. Won't happen again," she assured him.

He rested his hand on the small of her back as he ushered her to the door. "Good. Play along."

"Will do," she whispered, still lost in the kiss.

When they opened the door, Giovanni looked confused.

"Giovanni, this is my boyfriend, Nick," she introduced him.

"Really? I didn't think you had a boyfriend," he said, shaking Nick's hand.

"I do, but it's not Seb or Ethan. You asked if *they* were my boyfriend. They're not, he is."

"I see."

"Pleasure to meet you," Nick said, with his accent in full tilt. "Katie's told me all about you."

"Really? Because she told me nothing about you."

"He was who I was with for Christmas," Katie explained. "He lives in Sandusky."

"I see."

"Yep. I was running an errand for work when I thought I would drop by. Since I'm not over here all that often in my job, thought I'd surprise her," he said, and kissed her cheek.

Blushing in embarrassment, she felt for Giovanni, as she explained, "I don't get to see him too often."

"Is that an Australian or English accent?" Giovanni asked.

"Aussie, born an' bred. Came here after graduation an' started over in life. Ran into this beautiful shelia when me an' my mates were down at McGreggor's Sports Bar. Saw her a couple times before I approached her. She was there with her mates."

"And, how old are you?"

"Twenty-seven. I know she seems young, but she's mature for her age."

"That's seven years difference," Giovanni pointed out.

"Doesn't seem that way," Katie said, hugging his arms around her. He took the cue and squeezed her back.

"How long have you been together?"

"Only a couple of months," Katie explained. "None of my friends know about him, because I wanted to make sure we were going to continue to see each other. I didn't want to hear the griping and complaining about the age difference from them if it wasn't going to work out."

"I can see that," Giovanni said, satisfied. "They seem to be a little overbearing at times."

"But they mean well."

"All right. Well, do you want to ride over with me and Joey or are you two driving separate?"

"What if we meet you over there?" Katie suggested. "That way Joey's not going to feel put off by two strangers. We can talk in the restaurant in a more comfortable setting."

"Sounds good. See you there," Giovanni said, and took off for his jeep.

Nick opened the passenger door for her as he complimented her, "Good job. You didn't miss a beat and answered several connecting questions in his mind. How did you make all that up so fast?"

She shrugged in response, so he went over to his side and started the Explorer.

"Are you okay?"

"I just lied to him."

"Won't be the last time before this is over," he pointed out.

"And, I'll also have to lie to Seb when we get to the restaurant. Giovanni's reaction will be tame compared to the firestorm Seb's going to set off," she warned.

"It's part of the job."

"What a tangled web we weave."

"Just keep your story straight or Giovanni will catch it."

"I know. We're getting deeper, aren't we?"

"Yep. You think those snow drifts are deep, what we're walking into will be deeper than that."

She sighed. "Let it snow, let it snow, let it snow."

*   *   *

As they sat down at the booth, Katie heard a plate drop in the kitchen. She cringed on the inside, knowing it was Seb. Taking a deep breath, she stuck out her hand and introduced herself, "Hi, Joey, I'm Katie. And this is my boyfriend, Nick."

"Nice to meet you," he said, shaking Katie's hand. Then he shook Nick's as he hinted, "Have heard a lot about Katie, but nothing about you. Why is that?"

"Suspicious little buggar, aren't ya?" Nick quipped.

"Just cautious," he corrected.

"I didn't tell anyone about him until I was sure we would work out. Since Christmas seemed to be a part of contention with Seb, I thought it was only fair for everyone to meet him," Katie explained.

"Meet who?" Seb asked, walking up to the table. "I heard my name."

"Seb, this is my boyfriend, Nick," Katie introduced him.

As Seb shook his hand, he said, "I find it odd that I have not heard a single thing about you."

"As I explained to them, with our age difference, I wanted to give it a couple of months to make sure it would work out before I introduced y'all. Also, you wondered where I was for Christmas? I was with him at his apartment."

"Really? All day?"

"Yes. Ya got a problem with that, mate?" Nick challenged.

"Australian?"

"Yep."

"No. I just wanted to make sure nothing else was missing. Katie, did you not spend two hours with Giovanni in your dorm on Christmas Eve?"

"What does that have to do with anything?" Katie snapped.

"I want to make sure he knows what he's walking into," Seb said, nonchalantly.

"Exactly *what* are you insinuating?" Giovanni gave him a cross look.

He shrugged. "Just making sure everyone knows what's going on."

"*Nothing* is going on." Katie glared at him, the anger visibly evident on her face. "How *dare* you even hint toward something that is not true just to get under both of their skin!"

"Didn't you say Seb was a new friend?" Joey asked.

"He is," Giovanni acknowledged.

"With friends like that, bro, you don't need enemies," Joey cautioned.

"I only wanted to make sure everyone knew –"

"What I was doing?" Katie asked, cutting Seb off.

"She's not doing anything inappropriate," Nick jumped into the conversation, hoping to smooth things over before he lost the opportunity to get to know Giovanni and Joey. "As a matter of fact, Katie told me all about it Christmas Day. She said they ate dinner and played Texas Hold 'em. She said nothing happened, and I believe her. She's pure and will stay that way," he said, making his intentions clear to Seb.

"Are you saying you were with her all day and nothing happened?"

"Who are you, my dad?" Katie snapped. "Go have Dom take our order. I don't want to talk to you right now," she said, putting her hand up to stop him from saying another word. As he walked away, she added over her shoulder, "When you're more grownup, we can talk, but not before."

An awkward silence hung over the table for a few moments before Joey said, "Well, that was fun. Does this happen often?"

"No. Well, yes," Giovanni corrected himself. "Seb thinks he's laid claim to Katie, but she has made it abundantly clear it's not going to happen. And, now I know why."

"Sorry to make it such a shock. I was hoping to avoid all of this drama," Katie explained.

"It's okay. This is fun. I already know all I need to in just this little exchange," Joey explained.

"Meaning?" Giovanni asked.

"It's easy." He shrugged, crossing his arms. "She truly likes you as a friend. You've told me how she stood up to Seb, and I can see her doing that. Also, I can see why she kept the big guy a secret over there." He gestured to Nick. "It seems her other friends are extremely possessive."

"Yes. They are," Katie agreed.

"So, now that the cat's out of the bag, you can relax. I can imagine he's either in there calling or texting your other friends." He shook his head with a chuckle. "I would love to see her go toe-to-toe with Dad. You're right, she's just like mom."

"Think I'll take that as a compliment," Katie said

"As it was intended," Joey agreed. "You are a spitfire."

"Is that good or bad?"

"Well, you stand up for your friends and those close to you. That's admirable," Joey explained. "Those are great and rare qualities in a friend. You also don't take guff from anyone. That shows your attitude and strength. Yep, brother," he patted Giovanni's shoulder, "I approve."

"Thanks," Giovanni grinned, pleased.

"Tell ya what. I'd like to get to know you guys better, but I have to get to the gym. I'll go catch the bus and let you guys talk and enjoy your meal. Of course, you may want to consider switching restaurants since Seb is still steaming in the kitchen," he pointed out. "In the meantime, enjoy," he said, and slid out from the booth.

"Pleasure," Nick said, shaking his hand. "Have a g'day, mate."

"You too."

Katie shook his hand as well. "Thank you."

When he shook her hand, he bent down and kissed it. "The pleasure is mine. Keep an eye on the big lug." He nodded toward Giovanni. "He sometimes gets himself into trouble."

"Nothing I can't find my way out of," Giovanni huffed. "Go workout, you dumb jock." He playfully shoved him from the table.

With a smile and a twinkle in his eyes, Joey said, "Hey, one of us has to have the brawn."

"I'll take my brains over your brawn any day," Giovanni shot back.

With that, Joey was out the door.

"He's not as scary as you made him to be," Katie commented when the door closed behind him.

"He's not. He is a great judge of character and calls people as he sees them," Giovanni explained. "The problem with him comes if someone messes with him or the family."

"What happens then?" Katie asked.

"Hornet's nest is a mild term for it."

*   *   *

Once Dominic took their orders, and their meals were before them, the trio relaxed and enjoyed each other. Nick was impressed by the level-headedness of Giovanni. His heart was also evident. He saw why Katie liked him and fought for him, and knew Katie well enough to know her heart was in the right place. He decided it was going to be his job to make sure her heart stayed pure. He wasn't sure how long he would be able to protect her, though. While he would do all he could, he knew the real protecting would be up to God…and he trusted Him. He just prayed someday Katie would fully trust God as well.

As the trio talked, they heard a crash from in the kitchen. Seb came out of the kitchen a moment later, pale and shaken. He sat down at the table next to Giovanni and grabbed Katie's hands. When she pulled away, Seb explained, "I need to tell you something."

"You don't need my hands to do it," Katie snapped, crossing her arms.

He took a deep breath before he said, "Katie, Ethan called in a mess telling me there was an accident. He said he saw on the news that Aaron is dead."

"He's…what?" Katie asked. "What kind of accident?"

"May I?" he asked for her hand. When she gave it to him, he explained, "He was murdered in the Fenn Tower last night."

While she worked through some of the feelings through the day, the wound was still fresh. She couldn't help the tears that slipped down her cheeks.

He got out of his seat and crouched next to her. As he hugged her, he said, "I really need you to be careful. You're the only one of us who has talked to him since break. Seeing his face on the news sent another shockwave through the group." He brushed the tears off her cheeks as he said, "We don't want anything else to happen. Ethan said Cierra's coming back early. She can't handle losing Aaron too. If anything happens to you, it could throw us all for a loop some may not recover from. Please be careful." To Nick, he said, "While I don't know you, I'm going to have to trust that you won't let anything happen to her." Then he turned to Giovanni, and said, "And that you will use every resource you have to protect her as well."

Nick nodded. "I will."

"Me too," Giovanni agreed.

*   *   *

They stayed for another hour, talking about Aaron and making sure both Katie and Seb were in a good frame of mind before they left. When they pulled up to the dorm, Katie was still in thinking mode. "So, do you really think it worked?"

"What worked?"

"Do you think we pulled it off that you're my boyfriend story?"

"Pretty sure. I know Giovanni was more relaxed by the end of the meal than he was in the beginning. I also know helping you two with the loss of Aaron helped him to feel closer to you both."

"I agree."

"C'mon, I'll let you in," he said and got out of the car. He jogged around to her side and opened her door. She grabbed the arm he put out so she wouldn't slip on the ice. When they got to the door, he asked, "Want me to teach you?"

"You can do that?" she asked in surprise.

"Sure. Why not? It's a skill you'll need to know. Well, one of many."

"Okay. What do I do?"

He pulled the tools out of his back pocket, where they had permanent residence, and placed them in her hands.

"Yeah, okay, and *what* do I do with them?"

"C'mere," he said, and she stood in front of him.

When he put his hands over hers, warmth flooded her. He spoke in a low tone up near her ear as he explained what to do, causing her to have goose bumps. Speaking right next to her ear, he took her breath away, and her mind drifted to the kiss from earlier that evening.

"There," he said, cutting into her thoughts as he pushed the door open in a matter of seconds. "Think you can do it next time?"

"Uh, no," she said, certain her face was bright red in embarrassment.

"What's wrong?" he asked, concerned by her faltering voice.

"Nothing. I just…that seems difficult. I'll probably need a few more lessons."

"No worries. I'll get you to the point that you'll be able to pick any lock known to man in no time, like me. It's all in the finesse of the hands."

"They have finesse all right," Katie said under her breath.

"What's that?"

"Nothing," she said quickly. "Um, thank you for dinner and for letting me in."

"Want me to walk you up?"

"No. That's okay. There are agents up there," she reminded him.

"What about a little Texas Hold 'em? If nothing else, if Giovanni or Joey are watching the dorm, they'll think I went upstairs with you."

"Good point. We really don't know where Joey went."

"Nope. He could have come in here for all we know."

"I hope not," Katie said, alarmed. "That would be a major invasion of privacy."

While they climbed the stairs, Katie's mind raced. *Did Joey break in and check her room? How would she know?*

When they walked into the apartment, Nick said aloud, "Anybody home?" He had her stay by the door while he did a security check. When he was almost finished, Serrin came to the door. "Hey," Nick greeted her.

"She had company tonight," Serrin explained, walking into the living area.

"Joey?" Katie asked.

"Yep. He met Giovanni across the quad when you guys got here."

"Sounds like they previously set it up," Nick commented.

"I would say so."

"Did he take anything?"

"No. He did flip through her art and said, '*Wow!*' Is it really that good?" Serrin asked.

Katie left to get her sketch pad. She was frazzled by the events of the entire day, but didn't want the others to know. This was a level of heightened awareness she never felt before. "Here," Katie said, handing Serrin her sketch pad.

"Nice!" She slowly flipped through the pages. "These are fantastic."

"And, she doesn't take long to do them either," Nick pointed out. "She did this one in about forty-five minutes," he said, directing her to the drawing Katie did next to the pond.

"You know, we could *really* use you as a sketch artist. Maybe we should test you by describing someone and see if you can draw them from the description," Serrin suggested.

Katie shrugged. "Sure. Why not?" She sat down at the table with her sketch kit and pad. Nick and Serrin agreed on whom to draw before they described the woman to Katie. When she was finished, Katie held up the sketch. "Is this her?"

"Oh! Whoa! That's dead-on," Serrin said in amazement, as she looked at the picture of Agent Claire Brenner. "You weren't kidding. Her talent is amazing."

"Yep. Can I have that page? I'd like to show it to Seth," Nick asked.

"Sure." Katie tore out the page and handed it to him. "Now, what about a little Texas Hold 'em? If they're watching us, we should at least keep them wondering."

"Cheeky little buggar, aren't ya?" Nick smiled, relieved she was relaxing. He knew how thrown she was about Aaron, let alone the idea of Joey going through her room. He was grateful she would have an agent in the living room at night. Things were getting deeper as she waded into the Rossi family. Little by little, he realized her natural security was getting pulled from her. He prayed she would face this task with the ferociousness he knew was inside her. While he knew it was in her, he hoped she knew it as well…she was going to need it.

* * *

For the next week, Katie and Nick worked through the loss of Aaron. It took her a couple of days before she finally was able to tell Nick what happened on that night, and the conversations she had with Aaron the days leading up to his murder.

In the meantime, Nick and Katie also met Giovanni at the café for dinner. After the third time, Seb decided that Nick wasn't going anywhere and before he lost Katie he'd better accept Nick as well. From that point, dinners were much more enjoyable. Katie even liked how well Nick was fitting in. During that time, though, she was painfully aware she was being watched…and not just by the FBI.

"Um, I have something to ask of you both," Giovanni said, halfway through their meal on the day before New Year's Eve.

"What's that?" Katie asked, taking a sip of her lemonade.

"My father wants you guys to come to dinner so he can meet you."

Katie just about choked on her lemonade. Getting her coughing under control while Nick patted her back, she choked out, "I'm sorry. You want *what*?"

"My Dad wants to meet you, and asked if you would be willing to come to dinner sometime in the next week. Before the next semester starts, he wants to meet you and get to know you. Joey approves of you, and that intrigues him because Joey's hard to impress."

"Impress and approve are two different things," Nick pointed out.

"He likes you guys. Katie impressed him with her strength and you impressed him by standing up for her."

"I see. So, you want us both for dinner?" Nick asked.

"Well, I would imagine since her friends know, where one goes, the other won't be too far behind."

"This is true," Katie agreed.

"So, would you guys come over? It's only dinner."

"When?" Katie asked. "While I'm free since classes are out, Nick's work schedule needs to be taken into consideration."

"Well, you seem to get here by four-thirty. Is that normal?" Giovanni asked.

"Yep. I work from five in the morning to three in the afternoon," he said, eating a bite of his burger.

"What do you do, by the way?"

"Oh! I'm sorry. I thought we told you. We've talked so much, I guess it slipped through. I work down at the shipping yards."

He nodded in understanding. "That explains the early and long hours...not to mention the big build."

"Thanks, I think," Nick said.

"I didn't realize you never told me until my dad asked me the other day."

"No worries. It wasn't a secret. Honestly, I thought we told you. My bad."

"So, would you guys like to come over for dinner tomorrow night? Is that too soon?" Giovanni asked, hopeful. "To be honest, I want my dad to meet you so he'll quit asking all the questions. You see, for me to have a friend is rare. So when I do, he wants to know everything. It's not exactly fun by any stretch of the imagination, but it is understandable."

"Completely," Katie agreed. She looked toward Nick, "Will that work?"

"Sure. You said you lived in Bratenahl, right?" Nick asked.

"Yep," he said, taking out a pen and writing his address on the napkin. "Here ya go."

"We can be there for sure by five o'clock. With traffic, I don't want to commit to anything sooner than that and possibly be late," Nick said, tucking the address into his pocket.

"That'll work. I know it's a pain to ask, but he really wants to meet you for himself."

Nick waved him off. "No worries, mate."

"I have to admit that I'm nervous," Katie confessed.

"Why?" Giovanni asked.

"Because I've never been to a house that big. I wouldn't know what piece of silverware to start with. What happens if I make a huge error in manners?" she asked, slightly panicked.

Giovanni laughed. "Sorry, but if that's your biggest concern, then you'll do just fine. Most people would be nervous about meeting my dad because of what he does." He snickered.

"Just start with the outside and work your way in. Keep an eye on me and I'll give you hints."

"I'm going to have to take ya up on that one too, mate," Nick jumped in, knowing full well what silverware to use and when. "Being in the shipping yards, we're lucky if we get a fork and not a spork."

Giovanni raised an eyebrow in question. "What's a spork?"

"Oh, you have so much to learn, my friend. We'll teach ya the finer points of living in the middle class."

Giovanni shook his head, chuckling. He appreciated the candidness of both of them. When his dad originally talked to him about having them over, he was nervous, but they both seemed to put those around them at ease. He pushed his worries aside, confident it would be a breeze.

Chapter 8

Happy New Year

"You are not going to believe the night I had," Nick said with a grin on his face that went from ear to ear when he walked into the office the next morning.

Dakota looked up with a smile. He hadn't seen Nick this excited in a long time. "Spill it, Locke. You look like you're about to burst any way."

He sat down at his desk and placed the paper he walked in with face down. "Wait until everyone gets here. I don't want to have to explain it twice."

"Why do you look like the cat that swallowed the canary?" Todd asked, sitting down at his desk after grabbing a cup of coffee.

"Tell ya in a few minutes."

Claire walked in, looking like she didn't get any sleep at all. "Coffee. I need coffee."

Todd smirked. "Long night?"

"That's putting it mildly. Remind me not to go with Emma to a concert again."

"Really? You went with Emma?" Dakota laughed. "She's what, thirty-five now?"

"Yeah," Claire said, making a beeline for the coffee pot.

"And she out parties a twenty-six-year-old? That's pathetic."

Emma came in, ready to begin her day. "*She* is in the room now."

"Why is it *you're* so awake?" Claire demanded.

"I know how to sleep, my dear. They're called power naps. Now, around three this afternoon I'll probably need that coffee. But for now? Not so much."

"Unbelievable." Claire went over to her desk and dropped her head for only a moment before she looked over at Nick. "Why are *you* so happy this morning?"

"Got some great news," Nick hinted, drumming his fingers on his desk in anticipation.

"Good. I could use some," Seth said, coming in and sitting down at his desk. "Let's hear it."

Nick got up with the piece of paper in his hand and gave it to Seth. The others gathered around Seth's desk, looking over his shoulder. "Okay? I don't understand." Seth shook his head, confused. "It's a picture of Claire. What is this? Where did you get it?"

"Katie drew it," Nick said proudly.

"How could she? She's never met Claire?"

"Yeah. Why would she draw me?" Claire asked.

"Serrin Matthews and I described you to her, and she drew this. The kicker? She drew it in about fifteen minutes," he bragged.

"Really?" Seth said, now intrigued. "This is so detailed. It's incredible."

"Thought you would like that."

"I don't understand. Why is this important?" Claire asked.

"That's a side note. I haven't given the *real* news yet. Calm your brumbies, I'll get to it. In the meantime, a sketch artist of this quality could prove useful, yeah?" Nick hinted.

"Oh yeah!" Seth said, visibly impressed. He set it on his desk to take to Director Shaw later, and then looked up and asked, "And the rest of the news?"

"Well," Nick paused intentionally to keep the suspense, while the others dispersed to their desks, but continued to listen, "First off, I am now a part of Katie's life. She and I came up with a scheme where I'm supposedly her boyfriend…which I am not," he clarified, sitting down at his desk. "This gives me access to the college without raising any questions or suspicions."

"Is that what you meant?" Claire asked.

"Yep. Pretty intelligent, I think, which brings me to my next piece of news. You see, young Mr. Rossi has accepted me into his friend circle too, via Katie. Now," Nick put his hand up to stop Seth from cutting in, "for the third piece of news. Katie and I have a dinner date at the Rossi Mansion tonight around, ohh, five o'clock." He smiled in satisfaction as he propped his feet on his desk, crossed at the ankles.

"Are you serious?" Seth stood up in excited shock. "That's great! You'll have direct access to Rossi himself! This is working out better than I ever thought it would. Sweet! Great work, Locke!"

He grinned with pride as Seth gave him a high-five. "Thank you."

"News that was *well* worth the wait," Dakota agreed.

"Ladies and gentlemen," Brenda Birch came in from the personnel office, "I have a new temp for you today. This is Verna Kellogg."

"Is she going to last longer than the other one?" Seth questioned, referring to their streak of temporary employees.

"I certainly hope so. It would help if you guys weren't so hard on them."

Seth shrugged. "All they have to do is type and answer the phone. It's not rocket science."

"Though you would think so by their complaining," Todd quipped.

"I'm sure I can handle it," fifty-year-old Verna piped up. "I've been doing this longer than you've been alive."

"Oh! I like her," Emma said. "Feisty. We'll see how she handles the office."

"And let's not forget Agent Cyrus Walker," Nick added.

"Who is Cyrus Walker?" Verna asked.

Brenda sighed before she turned toward Verna and explained, "He's the director of Office Management. He seems to have it in for this crew, though I don't know why."

"Because we don't bow down to his pencil pushing highness," Nick explained. "He seems to think since he controls our office supplies, reimbursement forms, office furniture, etcetera, that he can say or do whatever he wants and we're supposed to bow down to him. And, if there was any doubt, that is *never* going to happen."

"Well, he hasn't met me yet either. I don't like to be pushed around, nor do I let the office I work with get pushed around," Verna said confidently.

Seth sighed. "Time will tell."

"According to her record, she's telling the truth," Brenda backed her up. "That's why I brought her to this office first."

"Why isn't she with her previous job?" Seth questioned.

"Because my husband got transferred and I go where he goes," Verna explained.

"And, what does hubby do?"

"He's a trainer for an insurance company. He got transferred here from Colorado."

"I see."

"Now you know," Brenda beamed, pleased by her selection for the office, "be nice to her and she'll take care of you."

"Sounds good," Seth agreed. He went over and introduced himself to her, "I'm Agent Seth Simmons, the agent-in-charge."

"I gathered that," she said, shaking his hand.

"Welcome to the team."

"I plan to stay," she told him.

"Good. We hope you do. On a side note, if anyone calls for anybody here, unless it's another FBI office, *or* from the DOD, take a message and tell them the person is following up on a lead."

"Got it," she agreed. "That sounds easy enough."

"You would think so." After the others introduced themselves, things settled down. "Okay, back to business," Seth said, sitting on the corner of his desk. He turned to Nick and reiterated, "You have a dinner at the Rossi's tonight?"

"Yep. Katie and I do."

"Is she going to be able to keep that temper of hers in check?" Claire asked snidely.

"Really?" Nick glared at her. "What is your problem with her? She got a door open we have been trying to get through for years."

She shrugged. "Just sayin' that you're Irish princess has a bit of a temper."

"Well, stop saying it."

"Yeah. She's a good kid," Dakota stood up for her. "When she does get angry, from what I've seen, it's in defense of someone else."

"Or because I stuck my foot in my mouth," Nick added.

"What is this group's obsession with her?" Claire asked.

"What's *your* problem with her?" Nick shot back.

"My *problem* is that we're trusting a very big operation to a twenty-year-old. This is a job for professionals."

Seth grabbed the picture Katie drew and put it in front of Claire. "This was drawn by a professional. Yes, she is young, but she's smart. She can keep her cool when she needs to."

"Yeah. She's like twenty going on thirty," Todd confirmed. "You should talk to her."

Claire shook her head. "No thank you."

"That's it!" Nick challenged her, "We need to talk. We can do it in here or in private. Choice is yours."

"Fine. Let's go down to the conference room," she agreed.

"I'm going too. You guys keep working in here," Seth said to the others before following them down the hall.

When they got into the room, Seth closed the door. While Nick paced, Claire sat down in a chair. Nick looked at her and said, "I know we have a past, but your animosity toward Katie is not warranted, nor is it professional."

She shook her head. "Our past has nothing to do with this."

"Wanna bet? Every time Katie's name is mentioned, you bristle up and start slamming her. For the record, *nothing* happened between her and Giovanni on Christmas Eve either. She's a good girl."

"And I'm not?"

"Not at the moment," he said, crossing his arms. "You sound like a jealous school girl."

"I have to admit he's right," Seth stepped into the conversation. "Your comments are uncalled for and just plain mean. She's a current member of our team. And chances are, when she finishes her two years as a police officer, I'm going to recommend her to Quantico. When she's done there, take a wild guess where she's going to land?"

"Are you serious?" Claire asked, stunned.

"Serious as a heart attack."

"She's too young."

"Not any younger than you were," he pointed out. "We took a chance on you, and that was a good decision by the way. Why wouldn't I request a brilliant, independent, young lady who seems to have a good head on her shoulders *and* who is a stickler for details? She sounds like a perfect candidate for our unit."

"And I can guarantee she'll have Director Shaw's backing too," Nick added.

"See, that's my problem. Why is everything getting handed to her?"

"It's not. She's being given a fair shot. If she handles this case as well as I think she will, she's going to get fast-tracked into here," Seth pointed out.

"Fine," she huffed. "Doesn't mean I have to like it."

"You're behaving like a spoiled brat," Nick snapped. He crossed his arms the same way she did and bobbed his head as he mockingly repeated, "Doesn't mean I have to like it."

She narrowed her eyes while she tightened her crossed arms.

"Keep it up."

"This still has nothing to do with you and me," she insisted.

"Really?" he scoffed. "Would you be giving her as hard a time if she landed on Dakota's or Todd's desk?"

"I don't think they could handle her. She's not the most compliant."

"She's more compliant on her worst day than you are on your best one," Nick shot, and then he added, "More mature too."

"Oh, like *that* was mature."

"Hey, fight fire with fire. You have to control your tongue and attitude."

"There's nothing wrong with my tongue *or* my attitude."

"Yes, there is. And, if you don't control it, I'll have you transferred so fast it'll make your head spin," Seth said, effectively stating where he stood on the situation.

"You're taking her side?" Claire looked at him in wide-eyed shock. "How could you? I was here first."

"There is no side in this. She's a co-worker. I have no idea where the element of competition is in this? You guys don't even have the same skill set. She only owns a computer to type her papers on and get emails. She doesn't even own a cell phone," Nick pointed out. "Technology is definitely *not* her strong suit."

Claire dropped her head into her hands, visibly upset.

"I got this, man," Seth said, seeing Claire breaking.

"I hope so, because I've had enough," Nick said and left the room. When he was in the hallway, he leaned against the wall and looked toward Heaven. In his head, he prayed, *'Father, I need a little help here. There are some lines dangerously close to being crossed that I don't know if I should even be close to. If it's in Your will, would you please help everyone through this, especially Katie? She's an innocent in this, but everything seems to be hinging on her. Tonight will be the huge break we've waited literally years to get. Please help it to go smoothly? I'm in Your service and in Your hands. In Jesus' precious name I pray. Amen.'*

Hearing Seth and Claire arguing through the door, he made his way back to the office, satisfied he made his point. He knew Seth would get things straightened out with Claire. He hoped she would stay around because she was a valuable asset to the team. He also knew Katie would be a highly valuable asset as well. Somehow it would all work out. He had faith.

*   *   *

Deep in the garden, in the peace of the night, Jesus knelt down to pray. The moment was at hand. In the twilight, He poured out His soul to His Father. With the final words, He concluded His prayer, "Abba, Father. Everything is possible for You. Take this cup from Me. Not what I want, but Your will be done."

An angel appeared to Him to strengthen Him. He prayed more earnestly, and His sweat was like drops of blood. When He finished, He left to look for His disciples, to find them asleep. After reprimanding them, He went back to prayer. This happened two more times, until in the distance, the group saw the band of men headed directly toward them with fire in their eyes, being led by one of His own disciples, a man from his inner circle…Judas.

* * *

Katie gasped as she sat up in her bed. The dream was fresh and the picture was cemented in her mind of Jesus praying in the garden. She pulled out her sketch pad and drew the scene, complete with the angel standing behind Him. Periodically, she would close her eyes as she drew to put the picture back in her mind. When she finished, she added color with chalk. The only things she added it to, though, was Jesus and the blood. The rest of the picture was left in black pencil.

When she finished, she tagged the bottom right corner with Luke 22:42-44, along with her name and the date. She then drove to the store and bought a frame to fit the picture. Upon her return, she placed the picture into the black frame and set it on her dresser, knowing exactly who it was intended for.

* * *

Nick by-passed the buzzer and picked the lock of the front door, walking into Katie's dorm. With the conversation between him, Claire, and Seth weighing on his mind, he understood this would be a turning point in their years of investigating the Rossi Family. He also knew tonight would be critical in proving Katie's value. If the two of them could get a comfortable foot into the Rossi family, Nick could take over the dangerous part of this assignment, effectively leaving Katie out of danger.

He knocked on her apartment door and Katie answered it with a grin on her face. "Why are you in such a great mood?" he asked.

"Stay here and close your eyes," she explained. "I have something I want to give you as a New Year's present since I missed Christmas."

"You didn't have to."

"Please? As you said, it's the giving not the getting."

"Right oh. I reckon I'd better let you. I wouldn't want to disappoint you with excited as you look," he said and closed his eyes. He silently counted to fifteen before she told him to open them. "Wow! I-I'm amazed. This is crazy good!" he exclaimed, looking at the framed picture Katie drew of Jesus in the garden. He ran his fingers over the glass. "This is stunning." He looked up at her and asked, "Are you sure?"

"Yes. When I finished, I knew it had to go to you. I had a dream about it and drew it."

"Kind of like when you dreamed about the fiery furnace?" he asked.

Katie's face went pale. "How do you know about that?"

"Serenity."

"I see." She gulped. "Are you telling me you went to my home town and talked to people I know?"

"Yes."

"What did you tell them?"

"Don't worry about it. We told them it was a fact finding mission."

"They didn't know I was even considering working with the FBI," she said, and started nibbling on her finger nails. "They must be really upset with me."

"No. They're concerned for you, so you may want to consider a visit before you go to Quantico. However, keep in mind that they will truly be happy if you're happy. They only want the best for you."

"I see."

"Anyway, I need you to clear your mind."

"Right. We're fixin' to go to a mafia leader's house. Nothing to worry about there."

He chuckled. "I enjoy your sense of humor."

"Twisted as it may be."

"Yes, twisted as it may be." He chuckled again. "I'm going to have to take you into the office and introduce you to the others. I'll bet you would get along with them," he said, and ushered her downstairs.

When they were in the truck and on the way to the Rossi's, Katie asked, "So, how does this work?"

"Meaning?"

"Meaning, are you wired? Are you carrying?"

"Not if we want to get out of there alive."

"What do you mean?"

"You don't think they're going to check?"

"What about in the car? What happens if we get into trouble?"

"The others are around," he hinted.

"Meaning?"

"Meaning, they may be in a truck, or a vehicle down the road. If we don't come out by a certain time, they'll come in and get us."

"I see. And, when is pumpkin time?"

"By ten o'clock. We're only supposed to be there for dinner and, if you remember, my cover states that I'm supposed to get up for work on the docks by five in the morning. The normal line of thinking dictates that by ten o'clock I should be on the way to drop you off so I can get home to go to sleep."

"Got it. Well, that makes me feel a little bit better."

"Don't be so nervous. You'll do fine."

"I hope so. I don't want his dad upset at me and make him stop being my friend."

"I doubt that'll happen. I'm pretty sure Giovanni will stand up for you. He seems to like you."

"I like him, too," she said, watching out the window as the scenery passed.

"What's on your mind?" he asked after a couple minutes of silence.

"Can we really do this? Can we free him? It's going to take something *really big* to get him to turn on his father and brother."

"This is true," he agreed.

"Along with a lot of time as well."

"Yep. It may take into next year. The point is to get in there and get information, which I can now do thanks to you if all goes well tonight."

"No pressure there."

He chuckled again. "Have I mentioned that you're the queen of understatement?"

"I don't mean to be. I'm just me."

He reached over and rested his hand on her shoulder. "And, who you are is who you're meant to be. That's the person we need for this job."

She suddenly sat up. "Oh my word!"

"What?"

"We didn't bring a gift," she said, panic setting in once again.

"Here," he said, and pulled into the parking lot of a store. "Let's go find wine or something."

It took them only a couple of minutes to find something appropriate to give to Mr. Rossi. On the way to the house, Katie packed it in a gift bag.

"Feel better?" Nick asked.

"Yes."

"Good. Maybe now you can relax?"

"Here's hoping. I usually don't have a problem meeting parents."

"Yeah, they all seemed to like you in West Springs."

"Okay, seriously, what's in that mega file you have on me?"

"I'll tell you someday. In the meantime, know we don't like surprises and are thorough."

"All right," she sighed, looking out the window again. When they turned down Giovanni's street, Katie almost fainted. "Seriously? We're going into one of *these* houses?"

"Yeah. What did you think?"

"I've never been in a house of this magnitude before."

"You'll be fine. Just remember, he puts his pants on one leg at a time just like you do."

"Yes, and is surrounded by big guys with guns."

"Pretend they're not there."

"Yeah, sure, ya betcha. That'll be a piece of cake."

"Good onya! That's the spirit," Nick said as they pulled up to the gate. They told the man at the gate who they were, and were let in and directed to the house.

The driveway seemed so long to Katie. "I feel like I'm going to an execution."

Nick put the Explorer in park. "No worries. You'll do fine."

"Here's hoping."

He got out and ran around to her side to open her door. "You balanced okay?" Nick asked, noting her foot slid a bit when she stepped out.

"I'm okay. I don't drink, but I could probably use one after this is over," she said under her breath.

Nick laughed again as they went up to the door and rang the doorbell. The butler who greeted them took their coats, and then a couple of men checked them for wires or weapons. Afterward, the butler escorted them through a couple large rooms to a sitting room where there was a fire going in the fireplace. "Comfy," Nick commented as they sat down.

"They will be with you shortly," the butler said before leaving the two of them.

Katie couldn't believe her eyes. It looked to her as if Giovanni lived in a museum by the sheer size of the home. It was definitely decorated by an interior designer. Uncomfortable was not a strong enough word for the way she felt. It was more like distressed.

"Quit biting your fingernails," Nick said, reaching over and lowering her hand.

"Sorry," she stood and started to pace, "this place is so big. It's intimidating."

"Pretty sure it's meant to be."

"What if I mess up? What if I do or say something that ticks off his dad and he won't let me see Giovanni again?"

"You're only meeting his dad. You won't mess that up. Be yourself. He won't be able to help but love you."

"I agree," Giovanni said, walking into the sitting room. "I see Girard has the fire going, so you won't be cold."

"Thank you." Katie blushed, embarrassed to know Giovanni heard her fears. "I didn't know you were standing there."

"That's okay. What do you think?" He gestured toward the house.

"I *think* this place is massive. I would need a map if I lived here."

Thankfully Giovanni laughed, taking it in stride. "I appreciate your honesty."

"It's beautiful, don't get me wrong."

"It's honestly a waste of space," Giovanni said. "Dad likes it because of the security, but there are times it drives me crazy."

"It didn't drive you crazy when we would play hockey in the hallways," Joey commented, coming into the sitting room. He shook hands with Katie and Nick as he continued, "We would get into *so* much trouble by scuffing up the hardwood flooring or putting holes in the walls, but Mom would always get us out of it."

"You played hockey in the house?" Katie looked at him in wide-eyed shock. "I got smacked around for saying something out of turn. If I put a hole in the wall, I don't even *want* to know what my dad would have done to me."

"Me neither," Nick said under his breath. In the process of their investigation, he found out what her father did to her and lost all respect for him.

"Did he hurt you?" Giovanni asked.

"Yes," Katie admitted. "That's why I don't go home anymore."

"Makes sense," Joey nodded.

"Still leery?" Giovanni asked Joey.

"No. Just a piece of the puzzle I was missing. It's all good."

"Good. Now maybe you can relax. Oh! I had our chef make my favorite, chicken parmesan."

"Sweet!" Joey smiled in delight. "He makes awesome bread as well."

"Dinner will be ready shortly," Lucca Rossi, himself, said walking into the sitting room.

Nick and Katie stood to greet him. As they shook his hand, they introduced themselves. "Thank you for having us over for dinner," Katie said, handing him the wine.

"Merlot." Lucca nodded in approval. "This vineyard is near Watkins Glenn, New York. They make a very nice wine. It will go perfect with dinner. Thank you."

"Our pleasure," Nick jumped in. "It was Katie's idea."

"I appreciate your thoughtfulness."

"And, we appreciate the invitation for dinner. Your house is gorgeous," Katie complimented.

He nodded in appreciation. "Thank you."

"Sir, dinner is ready," the chef, Marcus, said at the doorway. He looked at those in attendance, hanging on an extra minute at Katie. "Is this the young lady Giovanni has been talking about?"

"Yes, sir," Giovanni said, with his face slightly red.

"Welcome," he said before he asked, "Are you ready to head to the dining room?"

They nodded, so as they followed him through the house, Lucca told them the history of some of the antiques and museum art throughout the home. Giovanni was pleased to see how interested Katie was in his house. Nick was a tag-a-long as far as he was concerned. He didn't know him that well yet, but he adored Katie and hoped their friendship would work out. While he only had her in his life for a couple of weeks, he couldn't imagine going back to not having her in his life anymore.

When they sat down at the table, a server brought in a salad for each of them, along with fresh made bread, thinly sliced. When Katie took a bite of the bread, Giovanni couldn't help but chuckle at the delight on her face.

"This just melts in your mouth. If I lived here I would gain so much weight," Katie exclaimed. When the guys at the table burst out in laughter, Katie blushed. "I'm sorry. I meant to say —"

"It's okay. It's nice to see you appreciate fine food when it's served to you," Lucca commented, with a pleased smile. "So, how did the two of you meet again?" he asked Giovanni.

"I was in the library and asked her for help in finding books," Giovanni explained. "She not only helped me, but also taught me how to use the system."

"It's only taken you two and a half years," Joey said, tongue in cheek.

"I admit my shortfalls," he said in defense.

"Which are many."

"Boys, we have company," Lucca reprimanded. "You are giving our guests a bad impression of our family."

"Sorry, sir," they said in unison.

"Now, Giovanni tells me that you are not only from Oklahoma, but also an excellent artist as well," Lucca commented before he took a bite of his salad.

"Yes, sir. I'm from West Springs, Oklahoma. It's down near Oklahoma City."

"I see. And how did you discover Cleveland State from all the way down there? Are there no schools near you that would cover your major?"

"There are, sir." She nodded. "However, I chose Cleveland State due to the distance from my home. I did not want to go to a school near my house. My father and I are nowhere near as close as you and your boys seem to be…which is a pleasure to see, by the way."

"Why, thank you," he graciously accepted the compliment. "I'm sorry you don't get along with your family."

"It's only my father. My mother passed and we don't have any other family to speak of."

"Shame."

"It's okay, really. I'll do just fine."

"I'm sure you will. And you, sir?" He turned to Nick. "Where is it you are from? Is that an English, Australian, or South African accent?"

"It's Australian," Nick explained. "I moved here when I was seventeen to live with my mum's parents. They have a ranch in Wyoming."

"Beautiful country out there."

"Definitely."

"So, how did you land at the shipping yards in Ohio from a ranch in Wyoming?"

"Hate to admit it, but it was completely in error."

"Meaning?"

"I don't want to give you a bad impression of my family."

"I'm only putting pieces together of Giovanni's new friends," Lucca said innocently.

"Well, with all due respect of course, knowing how inquisitive Joey seems to be, it's no surprise that you would be the same."

Lucca laughed. "They are a delight, Giovanni."

"I know. I like them," he agreed.

"To answer your question, sir, I was angry with my parents for shipping me away to the middle of nowhere," Nick explained. "I left after graduation and never looked back. Through a wide variety of occupations, I ended up in the shipping yards. Then, by pure chance, I ran into this young lady at MacGreggor's Sports Bar a couple of months ago. And, the rest, so they say, is history."

"Sports bar?" Lucca asked with a disapproving look on his face.

"Yes, sir," Katie quickly spoke up, sensing the shift in Lucca's disposition. "My friends frequent there. I go to watch the games and enjoy the company, but I don't drink."

"I see."

"And, I go with friends from work. I don't drink either," Nick clarified.

"Good to know. And, the age difference between you doesn't bother either of your parents?" he fished.

"They don't know," Nick explained. "Neither of us are close to our family."

"So," Lucca sat back in his seat as the chef served the main course, "what is it you want from Giovanni?"

Katie looked at him in confusion. "I don't understand your question."

"Well, you know who I am and what I do. Where most people shy away, you seem to have jumped in with both feet."

Katie felt a twinge of anger. Biting her tongue, she said, "I'm not sure what you're insinuating." As soon as she said it, all of the men looked at her in shock. "I am fully aware of what you do."

"That's my question. In knowing what I do, why are you his friend?"

"*Because* of what you do."

"I'm afraid I don't understand."

"That's obvious," Katie quipped. Joey sat back in his chair with his arms crossed in delight as Katie went on – this was what he was waiting for. "With all due respect, sir, your profession has caused him to not have friends. People shy away in fear. They run the other way when they see him coming, which has caused him to be an outcast. I don't feel that's fair. He's a nice guy and I feel it's only right to give him a chance, *despite* what you do."

Lucca, taken aback by her words and audacity, said, "I don't believe you are being fair."

"Really?"

"Katie," Nick warned, "this is his house."

"That's okay," Lucca set his hand on Nick's arm, "I want to hear what the young lady has to say. It seems she has an opinion."

Joey snickered. "That she does."

Giovanni shot Joey a look while Katie went on, "While I don't know you personally, your reputation has caused Giovanni to not have any friends. I feel for him because he has a good heart, but no one will even look at him twice due to your, shall we say, activities."

Lucca burst out in laughter. "Oh! You are right, Joey! She's *exactly* like your mother. Speaks her mind."

"I don't appreciate being laughed at," Katie said, anger churning within her.

"I can assure you, my dear, we are not laughing at you. We are enjoying your spirit and passion," Lucca explained.

"Well, it doesn't feel that way. It feels like you were accusing us of being a friend to him with an ulterior motive. It also feels like you *were* laughing at me."

"Please accept my sincere apologies. I value my boys too much to not have all questions answered. We have ventured into new territory here. You are correct. They have not had a friend yet – neither of them. I have heard the reports of how you stood up to your friends for him, and wondered why. That's all."

"Because of his heart. He is a true gentleman, and I don't feel it's right that he has to fight tooth and nail just to have a friend. Speaking of which, since I'm on the subject, I don't feel that it's right for you to dictate what his major is without even considering his wishes."

"Really?"

"Yes. Have you even asked him what he wants to do?"

"As the eldest, it is his responsibility to take over the business."

"What if he doesn't want it?" Katie asked.

"That's not an option."

"Why not?"

"He is to inherit the business," he said, making it final.

"I see."

"What do you see?"

"I now see why he has not had any friends."

"Why is that?"

"Because you control every aspect of his life." As soon as she said it, Nick let out a groan as he dropped his head onto his hand.

"I now see why you didn't get along with your father."

The room froze. As the anger coursed through Katie's veins out of control, she stood. "My father drank to drown his feelings of losing his love. In turn, he took it out on me. It was not uncommon for me to have bruises and cuts on my body. I even ended up in the hospital at one point due to his temper. I can assure you, though, that it had nothing to do with my tongue."

Lucca stood, matching her stance. He only held his glare for a few moments before he snickered, and it quickly escalated to laughter of delight. He walked around the table to Katie and took one of her hands. He kissed it, and looked up at her as he said, "You have my approval to be a friend to Giovanni. You have no qualms about standing up for him." He glanced toward Giovanni and added, "This is a rare quality in a person."

"I understand that," Giovanni assured him.

He turned back to Katie and added, "You, young lady, are a true treasure. I appreciate your fire and passion. You are both welcome in this house at any time."

Nick turned to him, stunned. "Really?"

"Of course. If she will stand up to me, knowing full well who I am, I know she will do the same for him anywhere. That kind of loyalty is extremely difficult to find. When you do, you need to treasure it."

"I see."

"And, it's my understanding you stand up for the young lady just as much."

"I do."

"Then I know you will do the same for my son as well."

"I will."

"Then, you are both welcome."

"Thank you," both Katie and Nick said in stunned appreciation.

"I told you that you would like her," Joey interrupted.

"That you did. She definitely has a lot of qualities that your mother had. Treat her well, Giovanni."

"I will, sir," Giovanni said, relieved to finally gain his father's approval.

"And I will do the same," Katie agreed.

"Me too," Nick added.

Pleased, Lucca finished with, "I would expect no less."

*   *   *

Around ten o'clock, Nick and Katie left the Rossi home and headed back to her dorm. "Well, that went better than I expected," Nick commented. "You had me worried there for a few minutes. I'm not sure whether to kiss you or yell at you."

"Why?"

"I thought your tongue would get us into trouble."

"It didn't."

"You got lucky."

She turned from the window, glaring at Nick.

"What's *that* for?"

"For making me do this. We're gaining the trust of all three of them, only to betray them and get them to turn on themselves."

"It's to help Giovanni. Do you really want him to stay in the controlling environment he's in?"

Katie sighed as she looked back out the window.

"Well?" he asked after a minute.

"I don't know."

"Well, you'd *better* know. We need to stay focused."

"I'm in it so he can accomplish his dream."

"You need to remember that."

Katie only nodded in response, absentmindedly watching the scenery pass.

"You need to stay focused."

"I'm focused. I don't like the way we're doing it, though."

"Meaning what?"

"Meaning we're befriending a family in order to stab them in the back."

"We are not."

"Tell me you're not going to arrest Lucca," Katie challenged.

He glanced at her before turning back to the road. He understood he would need to tread this conversation with caution. "Our main goal is to dismantle the Rossi Criminal Organization, not to dismantle a family."

"In doing so, you *will,* or should I say *we* will dismantle the family, and in turn break Giovanni's heart. He doesn't want to see his father in jail."

"Are you sure?"

"Is that a joke?"

"Nope. He knows what his family does. He knows how his father handles his business. He's not ignorant. That's probably the number one reason why he doesn't want to take it over."

"Meaning?"

"People *do* die around them, mainly Lucca. This shouldn't be a surprise."

"It seems so old world. I have a difficult time wrapping my brain around the fact that this is real."

"Tell you what," Nick debated for a moment before he said, "I think I need to introduce you to the real world."

"What does that mean?" Katie asked, nervously.

"I think you need to come into the office. You need to have a realistic view of what's going on around you."

"Can I? I mean, am I allowed to?"

"I'll get a visitor's pass for you. I'll give you a call in the morning?"

She sighed. "All right. What do I wear?"

"Business dress will work, so dress pants and a dress shirt."

"Okay."

He pulled in front of her dorm. "Look, you're not in trouble or anything. I think you need to see for real what we're fighting. I feel the only way to do it is to show you what we face at work."

"If that's what you feel is best."

"I think it'll give you a new perspective."

"New Year, new view, yeah?"

"Yep."

Chapter 9

Cold Feet

The next morning, security called Nick to let him know someone was watching the dorm besides them. He called Katie and instructed her to drive to a mall parking lot and leave her car in order to see if she was followed. She was able to lose them before the garage, so she got into Nick's SUV there. He had her put her head down until he knew it was clear.

"Kind of scary. I've never had to dodge a tail before," Katie commented when she was able to sit up.

"If you're going to join the FBI, you'll have to get used to it."

"Why are you being so pushy?"

"What do you mean?"

"You keep saying, *if you join the FBI, you'll have to get used to it* quite a bit."

"Is it not true?"

"It is, but you are saying it with a 'get over it' attitude. It's said in a derogatory tone."

"Just trying to be realistic with you. Speaking of which, Seth wants me to take you to the shooting range today as well if we have time. I talked to him this morning and he wants you to start working on your shooting."

"I've never shot in my life."

"We know. That's the point. We need to get you working on that. He also wants to fast-track you, so I'm supposed to work with you on other skills as well."

"Why?"

"Because he wants you to breeze through the police academy, so you can fly through Quantico with no issues."

"He thinks I'm good enough to get into Quantico?"

"He thinks you have potential and wants me to make sure you make it through. You'll have to do a two-year stint as a police officer first, which Director Shaw said he's working with the Chief of Police to get done, but yeah."

"I see."

"Are you getting cold feet about working with the FBI?"

"No. It's just a lot to take in and process."

"Well, I know you accused me of doing it, but you really do have to get over it. You're getting a realistic idea of what goes on in our line of work. Are you okay with it?"

"Yes."

"Good, because we're here," he said, pulling into the parking garage for Nick's office.

"Very secure," Katie commented after a minute.

"That's the point."

"True."

"Ready?"

"Not sure."

"We have to walk into the front because we need to get you a visitor badge."

"Sounds good."

They breezed through security and were on their way upstairs in no time. "Well, that was easy," Katie commented when they were in the elevator about fifteen minutes later.

"That's because I was with you."

"Right."

The elevator opened up to the next floor and a couple of people got on. One of them nodded toward Nick in greeting. "Locke."

"Walker," Nick said in a cool tone.

"And, who is this with you?"

"Agent Cyrus Walker, this is Katie MacKenna," Nick introduced them. "Katie, this is Agent Walker. He's the director of Office Management."

"I see." Katie filed his name in the back of her head. "And, what *exactly* does Office Management entail? Do you handle personnel?"

"No. We handle office supplies, furniture, which team occupies what office, approval of expense vouchers, that sort of thing."

"So, you're kind of like a director of the stock room?" Katie asked, trying to figure it out.

Nick chuckled while Agent Walker cringed. "No," Agent Walker said, shoving his glasses up on his nose, "I'm in charge of office assignments and keeping track of office supplies."

"Oh. Kind of like a warehouse?"

Nick couldn't help it, he let out a laugh. Covering it quickly, he explained, "He, um, makes sure we have the supplies we need, tracks expenses, keeps us on budget, makes sure we have the updated computer systems, etcetera."

"Thank you, Agent Locke," Cyrus said, impressed, "I appreciate that."

"I didn't say you did a good job of it," Nick shot, hoping to take him down a couple of notches.

Agent Walker watched them get off the elevator with a look of shock on his face.

"May wanna close yer mouth, mate. It's not an attractive look an' there's no tellin' what you're gonna catch," Nick said just before the door closed.

Katie giggled. "*What* was *that*?"

"*That* was Agent Cyrus Walker. He's a bit too big for his britches, if you catch my drift. He relishes in the fact that he has control and feels we should do whatever he tells us."

"Hmm, sounds like the type of guy who needs to be humbled."

"He could stand to eat some humble pie," Nick agreed.

When they walked into the office, everyone looked up from their desks. Katie recognized some of them, but she also felt the chill from one of the women. "Who's that one?" she whispered to Nick.

"That's Agent Claire Brenner. The one you drew the other day. She's our computer genius. Why?"

"Because she either doesn't like me or you. I'm feeling a lot of cold from her."

"Really?" he asked, surprised by her accurate feeling.

"Yep. The rest are friendly."

"Mind sharing with the rest of us?" Seth asked.

"Just chatting," Nick dismissed him.

"So, are you *the* Katie MacKenna?" Emma got up and introduced herself. "My name's Emma Sharpe."

Katie shook her hand. "Pleasure to meet you." When Dakota and Todd came over to say hello, Katie commented, "Wow! Y'all look different."

"See, I told you that you should have waited to introduce yourself to her until you were dressed normal," Nick told them.

"Yeah, polyester is not my most favorite thing to wear," Dakota admitted. "I have to take allergy medicine to put it on."

"Pleasure to see you again," Seth said, shaking her hand. He took her over to Claire and introduced her. "Claire Brenner, this is Katie MacKenna."

"I know who she is," Claire acknowledged before she got up from her desk, leaving Katie's hand mid-air. "I have work to do," she said and left the office.

"Something I did?" Katie asked.

"No. She's got a problem with Nick," Seth dismissed her.

"Former flame?"

Dakota smirked. "She's good."

"She seems like someone who's been hurt," Katie observed.

"No, more like a spoiled brat who didn't get what she wanted," Nick corrected. He turned to Seth and asked, "Are you going to take care of that?"

"Definitely. Can you guys hold the fort while I go talk to her?"

They agreed. And while everyone else went back to business, Katie and Nick went over to his desk.

"Um," Katie nervously looked at the pictures of the girls, including Jill, on the dry erase board, "Why are those up?"

"To remind us of the monster we're looking for."

"I see," she said, sitting down in the chair Nick offered her.

"Not everything is peaches and cream here. As a matter of fact, most of it is not."

"Okay. So, why am I here?"

"Here's the file you asked for," Suzanna Barnes, the new temporary receptionist said, setting the file on the desk.

"Thank you." Nick accepted the file. When she was still standing there, he asked, "Is there something else?"

"Well, I was wondering what you were doing Friday? Ya see, there's this concert –"

"While I'm flattered, we're not allowed to date within the unit, so I'm afraid I am going to have to turn you down. However, pretty sure you can find another young gentleman willing to go with you."

"Thanks. I just thought…thanks anyway," she said, and went back over to her desk.

Katie watched her go back to her seat, and mentioned, "That was awkward."

"Welcome to my world," he said under his breath.

"I thought you had that older lady named Vera as your secretary?"

"Yeah. We really liked her, but it seems her hubby didn't like it up here and transferred them back to Colorado. We got another new one on Christmas Day, but she didn't last but three days, and now we have her. Anyway," he opened the file, "this is what we have on the Rossi family. This is top secret, so you cannot tell anyone what you know or you'll be arrested."

"Oh!" She looked at him, taken aback.

"This is serious business. There have been a lot of man hours and agents hurt or killed to get this information. This is also why I had you sign that non-disclosure statement."

"I see. I'll keep it to myself," she agreed.

"I don't normally show this to my charges, but I feel you need to see what they've done."

He took several hours to guide her through the file, showing her the many reports of money laundering, computer gambling, killings, kidnappings, bombings, attacks, and business dealings the office had collected of the Rossi family over the years, only taking a break for lunch. "So you can see how important it is for us to get in there and shut them down."

"I do," she said, with the photos in her mind of dead bodies at crime scenes, people in the hospital, and businesses blown up. "They're not very nice."

"Despite how kind and protective Lucca Rossi is of his family, I need you to see the wolf in sheep's clothing."

"I do now."

"Do you really think Giovanni has the heart to do this?"

"No."

"Do you really think if he's forced to do this, he'll continue to have the heart he has?"

"No."

"Then, do you understand why we have to take him down?"

"Yes."

"Will you help us and not fight me on it?"

"Yes."

"Good. Then this was time well-spent."

Anna-Sofia Santos from Agent Cyrus Walker's office walked in. "I have the expense vouchers," she said waving them in the air.

"Do we want them?" Dakota cringed, knowing he turned one in for an expensive pair of shoes that got ruined in a chase.

"Mmm, probably not, but you're one of my favorite offices, so let me give you a piece of advice," she offered.

"What's that?" Todd asked in amusement.

"It's in the wording. Here, like this one." She took one of the vouchers over to Dakota and said, "You need to reword this. It looks as if you're trying to get him to buy you another pair of shoes because you stepped in a puddle."

"They were expensive shoes!"

"Cyrus' question is, '*if they are so expensive, why did you wear them on a raid*'?"

"It certainly wasn't planned. And for the record, I don't do cheap."

"While I appreciate that, I'm trying to show you both sides."

"Can I see that?" Katie asked.

"Why?" Nick questioned.

She shrugged as Dakota brought it over. "I see her point," Katie agreed. "How about this?" she asked and reworded the way the report was written, showing the intent, the situation, and the reasoning behind the voucher for new shoes.

"That'll work," Anna-Sofia agreed. "Re-write this and I'll take it to him."

"Thanks," Dakota said grateful, and set to work writing a new voucher.

Nick couldn't help but ask, "I don't understand. Why did you do that?"

"When you see a problem, don't you want to help fix it?" she asked.

"I do, but why is it your business?"

"It's not. I only thought I would help. Writing is a strong-suit of mine," she explained. "Sometimes it's all in the perspective."

"Right oh." He sighed. "Well, are you ready to go back to your dorm?"

"If she's going to go back, and you had her car in a mall parking garage all day, she'd better have some shopping bags," Emma mentioned, not looking up from the report she was writing.

"Good point. Want to do some quick shopping?"

"Sure," Katie agreed.

They took the next couple of hours and went shopping for clothes for school before Nick dropped her off at her car. "I'll meet you at the dorm to take you to dinner."

"No need," she said, gathering her bags. "I'm going to eat in tonight."

"Why is that?"

"I have a lot on my mind."

"It's a lot to take in."

"That it is."

"Don't let it swallow you."

"I won't."

"Are you going to be okay tonight?"

"I'll be fine."

"All right. Do you want me to come by tomorrow for dinner?"

"That's fine," she agreed, and got into her car and left.

"Lord," Nick looked toward Heaven as she pulled away, "I fear for her heart. I want to help her, but I don't want to get too close to her. At least, I don't think I'm supposed to get too close to her. I don't know what to do," he admitted. "Lord, help me get her through this."

*   *   *

Katie pulled into her parking spot at the dorm and got out of her vehicle. "Where have you been?" she heard as she was pulling bags out of her car, and froze.

Slowly, she turned and saw Joey leaning against a tree with his arms crossed, hiding in the shadows of the night. As she stood, she nervously said, "Shopping. Why?"

"Because you were nowhere near your car for the entire day. Where were you?"

Despite her nerves, his demanding attitude set her off. "Excuse me?"

"It's simple. Where were you?"

"I was shopping. What business is it of yours? Were you watching me?"

"I was."

"Where do you get off watching me?"

"You are now connected to our family via Giovanni."

"So, that gives you the right to spy on me?"

"It comes with the territory."

"No. It doesn't. Does Giovanni know you're spying on me?"

"He understands you'll need to be watched."

"No. I won't. And, no, I will not answer to you as to my position every minute of the day. That is not happening."

"Would you like to discuss it with my father? The orders came down from him."

"Definitely!" Katie said, angry.

"This should be fun. C'mon, let's go."

*   *   *

"Katie just got into her vehicle with Joey Rossi," Agent Sadler said to Agent Serrin Matthews.

"She *what*?" Serrin looked up from her magazine.

"She got out of her car and looked like she was talking to someone. It wasn't until he came out from under that tree right there that I saw who he was. Then she got into her car, and she and Joey drove off."

"Oh, that's not good. Get ahold of Agent Locke immediately. I'm calling Agent Simmons," she said, dialing his number. "This isn't good."

*   *   *

"What do you mean she got into her car with Joey Rossi?" Nick asked, the color draining from his face. He looked over toward Seth, to see his head drop onto his hand as he listened intently to Serrin on the other end of the phone.

"She looked over toward a tree and next thing I know she gets into her car with Joey Rossi," Agent Sadler explained.

"And you let her?" he asked in shock.

"We didn't have a choice. It happened too fast."

Nick sighed, nervously running his fingers through his hair. "Right oh. I'll deal with it with Simmons. Keep an eye out and alert me immediately when she returns."

"Yes, sir," he said and hung up.

Seth hung up his phone and looked over at Nick. "What do you want to do?"

"With what?" Claire asked.

"Katie drove off with Joey in the car with her," Seth explained.

"I told you this would end in disaster."

"Shut your mouth!" Nick snapped.

"What? Don't like it when I'm right?"

"You'd better contain her or it won't end well," Nick warned Seth.

"Claire, shut up now or leave the room," Seth instructed.

"Fine." She sighed and commenced tapping away at her computer.

"While you're playing around with that thing, use it to search through the cameras in the city and see if you can figure out where she went," Seth instructed.

Claire sighed. "Five bucks says she lands at the Rossi house."

"Seth," Nick said, visibly on edge.

"Claire, no more comments. Just do your job."

"Yes, sir." She saluted and immediately got to work tracking Katie.

"What are we going to do if she ends up at Rossi's?" Dakota asked.

"Haven't figured that out yet." Seth got up and started to pace the room, deep in thought. "Do you have any ideas, Nick?"

"I say we trust her."

Claire clicked her tongue. "Really? Like she's done *such* a wonderful job of encouraging confidence so far."

"*Shut up!*" Nick growled.

"Last warning, Claire," Seth warned.

"Shutting up," she said, and went back to her computer. All one could hear in the office was the click-clacking of the keyboard under the fast fingers of Claire. "Found her," Claire announced several minutes later. "Surprise, surprise, she's headed toward the Rossi's."

"What do you want to do, Nick?" Seth asked.

Nick crossed his arms with a sigh and debated for a moment before he said, "We're going to have to trust her. We can't get any eyes on her."

"How long do we wait?" Todd asked.

"We could send a car to keep an eye out," Emma suggested.

"No. I don't want them to think she's being watched," Nick vetoed that idea.

Seth leaned against his desk with his arms crossed. "It's your call. You're her handler."

"I trust her," Nick said confidently.

"Then we'll keep an eye out until she appears again. Emma, call the dorm and make sure no one enters or exits the building from our end," Seth instructed her. "If they're watching the dorm, they will expect to see people buzzing around if she's being watched."

"But she is."

"We don't want them to know it. We're going to trust her to get out on her own."

"For how long?" Nick asked.

"We'll play it by ear and use the cameras as much as possible to see some sign of her."

"Right oh," Nick said, and dropped his head into his hands in prayer.

*　　*　　*

"It's a pleasure to see you again," Lucca Rossi said, sitting down with Katie in the sitting room of his home.

"Wish I could say the same."

"Oh? Is there something wrong?"

"Katie," Giovanni greeted her as he walked into the room and gave her a hug before he sat down in the chair up near her end of the couch, "Girard, our butler, told me you were here. I wasn't expecting you."

"And, I wasn't expecting to see your brother tonight."

"Joey? Where did you see him?"

"He was next to my dorm, demanding to know where I was."

"What do you mean?"

"I was instructed to keep an eye on her," Joey explained as he sat in the other chair near his father.

"Why?" Giovanni asked, stunned and confused.

"If she is going to be connected to us as a friend to you, she will need to be accounted for," Lucca explained.

"No. I don't. I shouldn't have to be watched in order to be his friend. You're taking away my security and freedom and I don't appreciate it," Katie snapped.

Noting Katie's body language, Giovanni stepped in. "I agree. Why is she being watched?"

"I want to ensure she is not working with the Rodchenko's," Lucca said.

"Are you serious?"

"Who are the Rodchenko's?" Katie asked, obviously lost.

"They are our rival family," Lucca clarified.

"I have no idea who you're talking about."

"That's obvious. Dad, you're going to have to pull your tail off her," Giovanni demanded. "She doesn't even know who they are."

"I have not let a single person penetrate this family in over forty years and I am not about to start now," Lucca defended his position.

"And I have not been anyone's possession, nor do I take kindly to losing my freedom just to keep a friend," Katie made her position clear. "I enjoy your company, Giovanni, but I will not let anyone take away my personal security."

"On the contrary," Lucca explained, "you are gaining security. If you are being watched, no one can hurt you."

"You are," Katie retorted. "You're having me followed and asking me where I have been if you lose me. You are not my dad, nor are you my guardian. I don't have to answer to anyone but God."

"I agree," Giovanni stepped in, feeling Katie may overstep her bounds with his dad. "I approached her. She didn't approach me. It's not fair for her to have her every move scrutinized because she wants to be my friend. That's not right."

"Your mother felt the same way at first, but she got used to it," Lucca said calmly.

Katie narrowed her eyes. "I *will not* get used to it."

Lucca was taken by surprise by her brazen attitude. "Young lady, I don't appreciate your attitude."

"And I don't appreciate you spying on me."

"There have been girls attacked on campus, have they not?" Lucca questioned.

"They have," she agreed.

"And, one of them was your roommate, correct?"

"Yes."

"And, didn't you just lose another close friend the day after Christmas?"

"I did."

"Would you not feel better knowing someone was looking out for you on that campus?"

Katie crossed her arms and glared at Lucca. "I will not give up my freedom for safety."

"I don't understand," Lucca was truly trying to understand her perspective. "Wouldn't you feel better knowing there are men looking out for you?"

"No."

"Why not? Help me understand."

"First off, you used the Rodchenko's – whoever they are – as an excuse to watch me. When that was debunked, you tried to manipulate me by claiming my safety was in jeopardy. Neither of which is true," Katie called him out. "The truth is you want to have control over me. You are using these two situations to watch me and keep track of my movements. I don't appreciate it."

Lucca dropped his head and sighed, shaking it. "You are quite a bit like their mother, stubborn and set in her ways."

"From what I understand, that's a compliment," Katie said, but stayed on edge.

"As intended." Lucca nodded, while he debated in his head what to say. "I don't like to be dictated to."

"And I don't like being spied on," she countered.

"I understand."

"Do you?" she pressed. "I don't want my every move watched. I don't want someone following me. I don't want to catch someone even in proximity of me. I understand if you are watching Giovanni, but not me. I don't want to feel on alert. I don't even want you to have your guys go deeper so they don't get caught." She turned to Giovanni and threatened, "If I find someone is following me, as much as I enjoy our friendship, I will discontinue it. Am I clear?"

Giovanni paced the room, running his hand nervously through his hair. Stopping in front of the fireplace, he crossed his arms. He sternly looked at his dad as he warned, "Dad, I love you, but if you mess this up for me, I will never forgive you."

His dad looked at him, taken aback by his assertiveness, especially since Giovanni was known for being passive. "I'm surprised by your attitude, son."

"Why? Through my entire life, people have stayed away from me because of what you do. When I finally get a friend, you sick your pit bull on her," he gestured toward Joey, "and you wonder why I'm upset? Seriously?"

"Pit bull?" Lucca questioned. "What do you mean?"

"Oh stop it, Dad!" Giovanni snapped. "You are not innocent. Knock it off!"

"Giovanni, I am not used to seeing this side of you."

"You'll see it more frequently if you don't call your dog off!"

"Dog?" Joey looked at him, offended. "I don't like being called a dog."

"Then don't be so obedient," Giovanni said snidely.

Joey sat back in his chair, wondering what direction the conversation was going to take. He decided to let it play out and stay out of it.

Giovanni glared at his dad and asked, "Are you going to call them off?"

"Yes," Lucca conceded.

"I mean it. If either she or I see someone watching her, I will never speak to you again."

"I understand."

"Katie, are you okay with that?"

"Of course. I want you to understand, though, that I don't want to lose my freedom in order to have you as a friend."

"Duly noted," he agreed. "Would you like me to follow you home?"

"No. I'll be fine."

Marcus walked into the sitting room. "Sorry to interrupt, sir, but dinner is ready."

"As upset as you were, would you kindly stay for dinner?" Lucca offered. "Please? Consider it a token of my apology."

Katie debated it for a moment before she agreed. "Thank you."

"Good," Lucca said, pleased.

Joey sat in his seat, surprised by the way both his father and brother reacted. His father stepped back when Giovanni pushed. Granted, Giovanni looked like he would have ripped his head off at the time, but it still stunned him that he bent to Giovanni. Giovanni was a big guy, and Joey knew eventually he would be taking over the family. Happy to see some spark of leadership finally in him, he looked forward to Giovanni taking over the family. His dad ran things the old school way, and Giovanni would bring in fresh ideas. Joey already knew he would lead security when he was of age. He half-wondered if Katie would eventually be a permanent part of the family as well.

Chapter 10

Arctic Blast

By the time Katie got back home, Nick was fit to be tied as he paced a hole in the carpet of his office. When his phone rang, he about jumped over his desk to answer it, "Agent Locke."

"Hey, Nick," Katie responded, calling him from the apartment where the agents were staying, in case the Rossi's were tapping her phone line as well. When she got home, Serrin explained what happened on their end and suggested she give him a call.

"Hey, Nick?" he asked, stunned. "All you have to say is '*hey, Nick*'? What happened to you?"

"Joey wanted to spy on me and I didn't agree, so he suggested I take it up with Lucca."

"Oh really? And, how did that go?" he asked, doing his best to keep his tongue in check.

"He agreed to call off his dogs when I threatened Giovanni if I saw even one our friendship was over."

"That was a big risk," he pointed out.

"But it worked and I shouldn't have to worry about being followed."

"So, do I understand you threatened to walk away if he didn't stop spying on you?"

"Yes."

"Even though we were already in? Do you know how long it took us to get this far? Do you realize what all you put in jeopardy?"

"Let me put it this way," Katie said, hoping to calm him down, "if I was willing to walk away, wouldn't that relax his dad a little more? If I was willing to bend, wouldn't that go against my character?"

"So, is it like a car salesman, where you're willing to walk away, so they bend and make the deal go your way?"

"Exactly," she said, relieved he understood.

Nick thought about it for a moment before he agreed, "Okay, I get it. It was a risk, but it worked, right?"

"Yes. It worked. Also, I found out just how much Giovanni didn't appreciate his father's antics."

"Meaning?"

"Meaning he told his dad if I stopped being his friend because he was having me followed, he told his dad he would never forgive him."

"Really?" he asked, pleasantly surprised.

"Yep. That tells me not only do I mean a lot to him, but I also mean more to him than his dad. He was definitely willing to stand up for himself as well."

"Yeah. That's huge."

"Thought you would like that."

"I get it. Just do me a favor and never take a risk like that again?"

"I can't promise that."

"Can I come over and talk?"

"Can it wait until tomorrow?"

"I would rather not."

Katie sighed. "I'm kind of tired."

"Fine. What time?"

"You can pick me up for dinner at four-thirty."

"That long?"

"I want to get some rest. It's been a long day."

"Fine," Nick gave in. "Have a good night. And, good job."

"Thanks," she said and hung up.

"Well, looks like you saved yourself on that one," Serrin mentioned after Katie hung up.

"What do you mean?"

"That could have ended badly."

"Why?"

"Once you're in the lion's den, you never know what will happen."

*   *   *

"You are not making it easy to take care of you," Nick said to Katie when he picked her up the next night.

Bundling up to go outside, Katie quipped, "Well, hello to you, too."

"I'm telling you that you scared me to death last night," he pointed out, as they walked to the truck with her clutching his arm.

"It worked out."

He opened her door for her. "You got lucky."

"I don't believe in luck. You shouldn't either," she pointed out when he climbed in the driver's side and took off for the café.

"What do you mean?"

"You shouldn't believe in luck if you believe in God. God is the One in control, not luck."

He nodded in understanding. "Fair enough. I was worried."

"I get that, but you have to trust me."

"I do. I'm scared for you, though."

"I understand. Remember, God won't let anything happen to me if He's not done," she said as they pulled into the parking lot.

He shut the truck off and looked over at her. "I made a promise to you that you would make it to graduation, and I intend to fulfill that promise."

"I get that, but you have to remember you are not the one in control."

Nick gave up the argument and escorted her to the restaurant. When they entered the café, they were greeted by Ethan. "Hey!" He grinned. "Surprise! I came back early."

"Ethan!" Katie squealed and ran up to him. He hugged her for a moment before he caught sight of Nick. Katie turned to see who he was looking at. "Oh! Ethan, this is my boyfriend, Nick."

"I wasn't aware you had a boyfriend."

"Really?" Katie said, skeptical. "You're telling me Seb didn't tell you?"

"Oh, he did. I'm only pointing out that I heard absolutely nothing about him from you, and then I get this call from Seb saying you suddenly have a boyfriend? I thought you were waiting until you graduated to date?"

"That was before I ran into him," Katie said, taking a step back.

"If you didn't want to date me, why did you keep stringing me along?"

"I did no such thing."

"Yes, you did."

"No, I didn't. I turned you down when you asked."

"And added that you didn't want to date until after you graduated."

"I also encouraged you to date others."

"Not really."

"You don't have to be around me if you don't want to."

"I do. Don't you understand that? Why are you being so stubborn?"

Nick decided he let the conversation go on long enough. "Is there a problem, mate?"

"Go throw another shrimp on the barbie and butt out of this conversation."

"Really?" Nick chuckled sarcastically. "Do you realize how ignorant you sound? No one really says that in Australia."

"Hop away, kangaroo boy," Ethan snapped.

"Back down, now!" Katie challenged. Anger was evident on her face as the green flashed in her eyes. "If you have a problem with my boyfriend, we don't have to be friends."

"Does he mean that much to you?"

"Yes," Katie stood her ground. "You may want to think through your decision as you consider that Giovanni isn't going anywhere either."

"This is ridiculous!" Ethan threw his hands in the air. "You're telling me you're willing to give up a two-and-a-half-year friendship over these two?" he asked, gesturing toward Nick, as Giovanni walked into the café at that moment as well.

"Oh, this isn't good," Giovanni commented, staying next to Nick. "It feels like an arctic blast blew through here," he said, rubbing his chilled arms. "What did I miss?"

"He's challenging her."

"Really?" Giovanni chuckled. "How's that going?"

Nick smirked. "It's interesting. I feel bad for whoever is on the other end of a discussion with her when she looks like that."

Giovanni rested his hand on Nick's shoulder. "Gotta agree with you there, brother."

"Well?" Katie crossed her arms.

Ethan sighed. "I don't like it."

"I didn't ask you to."

He debated a couple seconds before he said, "Fine. If I have to."

"Yes. You do if you want to keep me as a friend. I don't let anyone dictate who my friends are *or* who I date."

He sighed as he rolled his eyes. "Fine."

"Are you going to eat dinner with us?"

"I can do that," he agreed.

"Good. Maybe if you get to know them, you won't be so judgmental."

They enjoyed dinner, but it was tense. Katie was so frustrated, she almost left partway through diner, but she held on. Toward the end, she couldn't take it anymore and snapped, "You know what? I need to clear my head. I'm going to walk back to my dorm."

All three guys at the same time shouted, "NO!"

As soon as they said that, she stood from the table. Throwing her napkin down, she stormed out of the restaurant in a huff.

"We need to follow her," Nick said, and got up, closely followed by Giovanni and Ethan.

When they caught up to her, Nick demanded, "Where do you think you're going?"

"Seriously?" Katie looked at him, stunned.

"You can't go running around out here by yourself," Nick yelled at her. "There's a murderer and a rapist out here, along with the fact that you're in downtown Cleveland after dark. Do you seriously think we're going to let you go by yourself?"

"Do you seriously think I'll let you tell me what to do? You're not my dad!"

"No, but I love you!" he shouted...leaving a stunned silence.

Katie stood there, dumbfounded. *Was he serious or was he pretending?* "You can't be –"

He cut her off with a passionate kiss, right in front of both Ethan and Giovanni. She resisted for a couple of moments before she gave in and returned the kiss, melting in his arms.

She barely heard the whistles from Giovanni and Ethan as Nick and Katie pulled away from each other.

"Yeah, I'd say that's real," Ethan observed.

"I could have told you that. Are you blind? Did you miss the way they looked at each other through dinner?" Giovanni asked.

"You mean you're not interested in dating her?"

"No. Why would I? I'm happy and content to be her friend. You, on the other hand, seem to keep pushing her."

"Really?" Ethan turned to Giovanni with his arms crossed.

"Knock it off," Katie said, not taking her eyes off Nick's, who was lost in hers as well.

"What do you mean?"

Still looking at Nick, she asked, "Can I catch the two of you tomorrow? Kind of need to talk to Nick tonight."

"Sounds good," Giovanni agreed. "Looks like you two have a lot to talk about. C'mon, man," he said, gently tugging on Ethan's arm. Ethan hesitated for a moment before he left with him.

"Was that real or for their benefit?" Katie asked when they were out of earshot.

"I do love you…." When she took a step back, he clarified, doing his best to convince himself, "Like a sister. You're my charge. I'm your handler. The reason I kissed you was to give our relationship credibility. If they never see us kiss, they won't believe it."

She crossed her arms and let out a slow, deep breath before she responded, "I see."

"I don't think you do. I'm afraid for you for so many reasons, with the most important one being your eternal security."

"That's my decision that I will make in my own time."

"With everything going on and your nonchalant attitude toward the dangers around you, I have to tell you that you terrify me. You're a good girl, but you and I both know that's not enough."

"Let God direct and guide."

"Why is it you trust Him with everything except your eternal security?"

Katie thought for a moment before she slipped her arm through his and they made their way to the dorm while they talked. "I don't know how to answer that."

"Why not? You have the faith. You're doing the work. I know you know your Bible and have a heart for Him. I don't understand why you're misfiring when it comes to leaping in?"

"I guess it's my stubborn streak."

"Oh! For crying out loud!" He turned to face her, resting his hands on her shoulders. "Is that your excuse? You have got to get over yourself. You're not in control. You told me yourself that God is the one who is in control. What was it you said? Oh yeah. '*You can't believe in luck if you believe in God.*' Well, believing in God and trusting in God are two different things. You believe He exists, but do you trust He is the Sovereign One? Do you believe Jesus is the one and only way to Heaven? Do you believe He is the Son of God? Do you believe He gave His life for you on the cross to pay the penalty for your sins? Do you believe in the leading of the Spirit?"

"Yes."

"No!" He growled. "You believe in that here," he said pointing to her head. "But, do believe in Him here?" He asked, pointing to her heart.

"Good question."

"Do you have a good answer?"

"That's what I need to work on."

"May want to think about that one a little quicker. You've put yourself in some scary positions lately," he pointed out.

"I don't want to do it just because I don't want to go to Hell. I want to do it because I believe and trust in Him."

"Are you saying you don't?"

"I don't know."

"You talk a good talk, but is it genuine?"

"That's the question."

"Well, you'd better figure out the answer before it's too late," he warned as he unlocked her dorm. "Sweet dreams and we'll talk tomorrow, okay?"

"Okay. Thank you."

"My pleasure," he said before he kissed her cheek. "I gotta go." As he left for the café to get his SUV, he prayed for Katie once again for safety, security, and a sound mind to make the right decision.

*   *   *

From where Joey stood, glancing around the corner of the dorm from Katie's in the shadows of the trees, he could clearly see Katie and Nick. He knew he wasn't supposed to be watching her, but he and his dad agreed to keep an eye on her to see if she got herself into trouble.

He still wasn't sure about Nick, until the kiss. Seeing the passion in that kiss told him all he needed to know…Nick was in love with Katie. Once Nick left, Joey disappeared as well, to report back to his dad. Yes, Nick didn't kiss her on the lips before he left her at the dorm, but they were in a rather heated argument, so it surprised him that he kissed her at all.

He hoped one day to find a girl that he could love as much as Nick loved Katie. Truth be told, he admired Katie, and only wanted the best for her. His dad had a firm belief that Nick was only temporary, and that eventually she and Giovanni would get together…confirming Joey's thoughts as well.

*   *   *

On the way up the staircase, the conversation between her and Nick weighed heavily on Katie's mind. She challenged God and He answered. *What was holding her back?*

"Great!" Katie sighed as she entered the second floor staircase, where a light was blown. "Seriously? I know it's break, but good grief! Can't anyone change a light bulb in here?"

"I unscrewed it," she heard and froze in fear. Feeling her pulse in her throat, she couldn't speak a word. From out of the corner of the dark staircase, a tall figure in all black, with a hooded sweatshirt, grabbed her with one arm while he put a cloth to her mouth with the other. "Seems there are others in the dorm who may hear you if I didn't take you out here," he hissed near her ear.

The last thing she saw before her eyes closed was the light shining down the staircase from the third story. She was in trouble…and she was on her own!

Chapter 11

Put On Ice

"Serrin?" Agent Keller asked, while she rested on the couch of their hideaway apartment down the hall from Katie's.

"Yeah?"

"Um, Agent Locke dropped Katie off quite some time ago."

"Really? Why didn't you tell me she was in her apartment?"

He turned to face her with a slight twinge of concern. "Because she hasn't gotten to her apartment yet."

She sat up in alarm. "How long ago did he drop her off?"

"A good ten minutes. Even if she was dawdling up the stairs, she should have been up here by now."

"Keller, you keep an eye out. We don't want to sound any alarms if she just fell or something. Bryant, you're with me," she said to the two agents in the room as she removed her pistol from its holster on her waist.

They cautiously went down the hall to the staircase, keeping an eye out in every direction, pistols ready. "Matthews?" Came over the radio from Keller.

"Go ahead," Serrin answered.

"There's a truck pulling away. It's been there all day for cleaning the carpets, but it just pulled away."

"Where?" Serrin asked, her heart rate pulsated rapidly.

"North entrance. I'm calling Locke."

"Please, and thank you," she said, and they both sprinted to the north entrance of the dorm. They ran out in time to see the truck skidding its way out of the parking lot toward the entrance of the school. "Get Wolfe on the radio!" Serrin yelled to Keller. "They're headed toward the gate house."

*   *   *

"They're what?" Dakota asked. He looked up in time to see the truck speeding toward the gate and it plowed through, leaving the gate in splinters. "Lord, help her! You guys better get Locke and Simmons…fast!"

"I already alerted Simmons. I'm contacting Locke next."

"Copy," he said and put his radio down. He sighed before he looked toward the sky, "If You're really there like Nick says, Katie needs Your help. Please look after her?"

*   *   *

Nick hung up the phone, his face pale. He growled in anger as he pounded the steering wheel. "Bloody hell! Why now?"

He dropped his head onto the steering wheel for a moment when his phone chirped. He glanced at the phone to see it was Seth. "Locke," he answered.

"What happened? The campus agents are in a frenzy. All I could get was something about Katie and a work truck."

Nick sighed, beside himself. "Someone took her."

"Who?"

"I don't know."

"Well, you'd better find out! Get your tail end in here!" he roared before the phone went silent.

"Yes, sir." Nick threw his phone on the seat next to him. He looked toward God and said, "You know, it's days like this that truly test my faith in You. She's close. Why have something happen to her now? I don't understand. Why?"

Isaiah 55:8 and 9 came to his mind, *"For My thoughts are not your thoughts, neither are your ways My ways,"* declares the Lord. *"As the heavens are higher than the earth, so are My ways higher than Your ways and My thoughts than your thoughts."*

"I don't understand this situation, but I *will* trust You," Nick said, and drove to the office as quickly as he could. "I don't have a choice."

*   *   *

Nick strode purposefully into the office and pointed a finger at Claire. "You say one word and you *will* regret it. Do we have an understanding?"

"The only thing I want to say is I hope we find her. I've been searching the cameras since Seth called me in. It seems he drove the truck into a parking deck, that's where I lost them. By the time the agents got there, the truck was abandoned."

"But evidence of Katie was left behind," Seth said, coming into the office with a folder in his hand. "Seems he wrapped her in a carpet to get her to the truck. That's why the agent didn't catch it until it was too late."

Nick stood there, unsure of what to say. He was pleasantly surprised by Claire's change in disposition, but disturbed by the circumstances. He prayed with every bone in his body God would help him find Katie and she would be okay.

*   *   *

By three o'clock in the morning, all leads were dry. "We have one more option," Nick looked up from where he was resting his head on his desk.

"What?" Seth asked.

"The Rossi's."

"Wait. You want…are you saying what I think you're saying?"

"What if Joey took her? He took her before."

"Of her own free will."

Nick stood up and grabbed his coat off the back of his chair. "One way to find out."

"Wait a second. You guys need to change first."

"Who?"

"Take Todd and Dakota with you. You're going to have to change first, though, because you guys are supposed to be dock workers," Seth pointed out.

Dakota shook his head. "I can't. Giovanni's seen me on the campus as security. I've already talked to him. You're going to have to go."

"Fine. I'll go. We'll meet at the dorm in twenty minutes?" Seth asked, checking his watch.

"Sounds good," Nick said, already half-way out the door.

"This should be fun," Todd commented to Dakota. "A crime family and the FBI joining forces?"

"Not necessarily. Nick's thinking Joey has her. I highly doubt he would work with them. He's not that desperate yet."

"*Yet*," Todd reiterated.

*   *   *

Nick was pounding on Ethan's door by a quarter to four in the morning. "What are you doing here at this hour?" bleary-eyed Ethan demanded.

"Can we come in?"

Ethan, who was in the middle of a sleep cycle as he stumbled clumsily to the door, focused his eyes to see two other guys with Nick. They looked pretty rough, so he let them in. "I didn't do anything," Ethan said as they walked in.

"Katie's missing. When was the last time you saw her?" Nick asked.

"Wait. She's *what*?" Ethan wavered, stunned by the news. "The last time I saw her was with you. What did you do?"

"Nothing. Security let her in. That was the last I saw her. I tried calling her when I got home like I always do so she doesn't worry. When I did, she didn't answer," Nick lied. "I kept calling every hour and finally couldn't take it anymore, so I came with my buddies. We tried knocking and when she didn't answer, we kicked the door in. She's not there. Her bed isn't even disturbed."

Ethan slowly sat down in his chair, hoping to gather some semblance of a thought. "I don't –" He dropped his head into his hands, shaking it, doing his best to keep himself composed. Looking up at Nick, he pleaded, "We have to find her. I don't want to bury another friend. I can't. First Jill, then Aaron, now…I just can't. Do you understand me?" he asked, the fury solidifying on his face, as fear and anger fought for control of his emotions. He stood, shocked into coherency. "Where do we start?"

*   *   *

The four men pulled up to the Rossi gate house. "Can I help you gentlemen? Are you lost?" an armed guard asked, as another had a weapon pointed toward their vehicle.

"We need to see Giovanni," Nick said. "Please tell him it's Nick and something's happened to Katie. It's an emergency."

"It had better be. It's four-fifteen in the morning." He reluctantly got on the phone with the main house. The butler woke Giovanni, who got on the phone with the guard. He cleared them all to come in.

"This is where Giovanni lives?" Ethan asked, amazed by the size of the house.

Nick smirked. "Yeah. May wanna close your mouth, mate. It looks even bigger inside."

"This place is massive!"

"Yeah. I know. Been here before. Now, just so you know, they will check you for any weapons. If you have them, leave them in the car," he said to all three guys.

To Ethan's shock, Todd and Seth put their guns in the glove compartment. "Hey, you don't go into downtown Cleveland in the middle of the night without a weapon," Seth explained, hoping to put his mind at ease.

Todd shrugged. "Yeah. That's just common sense."

"I guess I never thought about it," Ethan admitted.

Nick slapped Ethan's arm. "Get yourself together. I need you to be alert."

"For what?"

"Anything."

*   *   *

After everyone introduced themselves, Giovanni asked, "I'm sorry. What's going on?"

"I dropped Katie off at the dorm, but she never made it up to her room," Nick explained, while he and the guys were frisked by Giovanni's men.

"What do you mean? How do you know?"

"Because we kicked the door in."

"Oh," Giovanni said, taken aback. He glanced over his shoulder when he heard someone on the stairs.

"What is going on down here?" Lucca demanded. "It's almost four-thirty in the morning. Is this some sort of college prank?"

"No, sir," Nick spoke up. "We need your help. Katie's missing."

"What do you mean by missing?"

"I dropped her off after dinner tonight, and when I got home, I called her and got no answer. I have tried for hours before I called a couple friends of mine to come help me look. Downtown Cleveland in the middle of the night is not safe, and Katie's somewhere in it. You guys haven't heard from her, have you?" Nick asked, worry and fear evident on his face.

Lucca finished his way down the stairs and introduced himself to Ethan, Todd, and Seth before he turned to Nick. "I'm sorry to say, we have not seen her today. She was here yesterday, and I believe she ate dinner with Giovanni and you tonight."

"Yes, sir," Nick confirmed.

"How can we help?"

"Well, I know she has come here with Joey before. Would you mind asking him if he saw her?"

"He'd better not," Giovanni glanced sideways at his father, who shook his head.

"If he did, I can assure you it's not from me. Girard, would you mind waking Joey?" he asked the butler.

"Yes, sir," Girard said, and left the group.

"Is there anything to go off of?" Lucca asked.

"No. The security guard said a truck went flying through the gate around six-thirty tonight at a high rate of speed," Todd explained. "We checked there after we went to her apartment."

"I see." Lucca nodded, mentally filing the information. "Anything else?"

"Not right now. I know you have certain connections that could be helpful," Nick said, desperate.

"Are you asking for my help?"

Nick nodded. "I could go to the police, but I know time is of the essence."

"This is true. And, according to your timeline, the criminal potentially has an almost ten hour jump. The first twenty-four hours are the most crucial. I will help," he said, shaking Nick's hand.

Relieved, Nick agreed, "Whatever I can do, please let me know."

"What's going on?" a sleepy Joey asked, coming down the stairs.

"Have you pulled your men off Katie?" Lucca asked.

Joey rolled his eyes. "This again?"

Lucca got a cross look on his face, and demanded, "Did you, or did you not pull your men off Katie?"

Joey's eyes widened in surprise. "Yes, sir. You told me to pull them off last night. Why?"

"She's missing."

"She's *what*?" His heart rate exploded. He knew Katie went into the dorm, but he couldn't tell them that. While he pulled his guys off watching Katie, he had kept an eye on her. If Giovanni found out, he would be furious with Joey and his dad.

"Missing."

"Why? Wait. What?"

"Katie is missing, you moron!" Giovanni snapped. "Wake up!"

"Why is it my fault she's missing?" Joey growled.

"Where were you tonight?"

"Working out with Dante and Sal. Why are you accusing me?" he yelled.

"Because you haven't liked her from the start."

"Because she's not one of us."

"She doesn't have to be!" Giovanni yelled. "That's one of the things I appreciate the most about her." He stopped and took a deep breath with his hands on his hips. Looking up the stairs toward where Joey remained, he explained, "It's her innocence. It's the fact that I don't have to have to pretend to be something I'm not around her. I can be myself. Why don't you get that?"

Joey pounded on the bannister. "I do! I only worry about you. I don't want to get a knock on the door someday to find out that it's *you* who's missing. Don't *you* understand that? I don't want to have a cop come and tell us that you're dead, like they did with mom."

Silence awkwardly hung in the air. No one said a word or moved a muscle. Finally Lucca spoke, "Boys, I love you. I also adore Katie, who is our priority at the moment. Joey go call the boys and get them over here. Girard, wake Marcus and have him make breakfast. We start in thirty minutes," he said and left up the stairs, Joey close behind.

"What do we do?" Nick asked.

"You go to the sitting room. Someone will come get you when we're ready," Giovanni said. "It's this way."

After he left them in the sitting room for upstairs, Seth asked Nick, "Do you trust them?"

"We have to," Nick said, practically a whisper. "Right now they're our only hope." He, Todd, and Seth knew their team was doing what they could from their end. This was an opportunity to work with the Rossi's and see how their organization functioned, and how entrenched they were within the system.

*　　*　　*

"I don't understand. How did you get this?" Nick asked as they watched the footage from the parking garage. They had already watched video from the campus where the truck left the dorm and then when it went through the gate.

"I have my ways. Now," Lucca pointed toward the truck, "it seems, due to the attacks on campus, the FBI have joined the police in this investigation. They have already been alerted and have tracked this vehicle down. It is in their possession."

"What can we do?" Seth asked.

"The truck was stolen," Lucca went on. "There are no fingerprints in the truck either."

Seth forced the vomit down that wanted to come up as his stomach lurched. *How was he getting this information?*

"It seems that young Katie was wrapped in a carpet of some kind. That is how she was carried from the dorm," Lucca continued. "They found her hair on the carpet."

"You have the carpet?" Todd asked.

"No. The FBI have it in their possession."

"I see."

Nick was dumbfounded on the extent of information Lucca had. "That's all fine and dandy, but what can we do to find Katie?"

"Patience," Lucca said, resting his hand on Nick's shoulder. "Time will tell."

"What do we do in the meantime?"

"Pray, my good man. Pray."

*   *   *

Katie moaned as she struggled to open her eyes. When she did, all she saw was darkness. She instantly felt the frigid temperature in the room and smelled the must and mold. The iciness of the metal bed rails sent a chill down her spine. When she shivered, she noticed her coat was gone, along with her shoes and socks. There was also no heater in the room.

As her eyes adjusted, she saw the handcuffs on her wrists, which were attached to the brass bed post. Seeing a quilt on the bed, she pulled it with her bare feet until her hands could reach it. She then tucked it around her body as well as possible.

After a while of sitting on the bed, her body on high alert, the sun finally peeked through the window, showing streams of light into the room. She gasped as she looked around. The brick walls were covered with pictures of her! Everywhere she looked, she saw memories of her time at the college. Some of her drawings from class were even on the wall. She shook her head, alarmed as to what would possess someone to do this. That's when she had the realization. The girls attacked looked like her, because the attacker wanted her. Aaron was also wearing her hat and scarf the night he was killed. With his long hair, he must have looked like her from the back. Tears formed in her eyes and her heart broke when the thought struck her that Jill and Aaron died ultimately because of her.

*   *   *

"We have to get away from him to get into the office and find out what's going on," Seth whispered to Nick around lunch time.

"I know. Let me see what I can do."

"Is something wrong?" Lucca asked.

"They need to work, but want to help look for Katie. I can't go to work with what I have going through my mind right now."

"Understandable," Lucca consoled him. "Know everything possible is being done. Gentlemen, if you would like, my driver, Ignacio, will drop you off anywhere you like."

"Actually, that would be great," Seth said, in appreciation. "If he could get us to the docks, that would be awesome. We can still get in a couple hours before we have to go home."

"My pleasure. You are welcome to return this evening. I have already instructed Marcus to have a continuous buffet going for those looking," Lucca explained.

"Keep us posted, brother. We'll be back later," Seth patted Nick on the back.

"They'll find her," Todd encouraged. "Between them, the FBI, and the police, I'm sure they'll find something."

"I can only hope," Nick said. "The more time passes, the chances of finding her diminish."

"We *will* find her," Lucca promised. "I assure you of this. Our best men are on it."

"Thank you," Nick said, feeling as if he made a deal with the devil.

Chapter 12

Frosty

"Talk to me, people!" Seth walked into the office with Todd a couple hours later. The room was buzzing with over twenty people from other units, as well as Emma, Dakota, Claire, and Director Shaw.

Claire got up and turned on the overhead screen, which was attached to her computer. "There are fifteen other people in her dorm. Originally there were only five, but others have been returning over the last week. Having said that, we've been able to account for all of them. They were either at work or the cameras placed within the dorm at the end of the halls had them in their apartments at the time of the kidnapping, so they are all cleared," she said, clicking through several scenes from the dorm. "Due to the break, many of the businesses around the campus are temporarily closed. A lot of them use the college students as employees. With them not there, they were on skeleton crews. Also, they depend on the college for business. Now, within those businesses around the college, there are only a couple places Katie frequents. The main three are the grocery store, book store, and the café. I hacked into the camera systems of the store since it's attached to their main computer, and it shows the owner, Erich Berliner, was at the store at the time of the kidnapping," she said, showing the photo. "The bookstore is shut down since it's break. That leaves the café, which we don't have a camera for. The main ones working there since break are Riccardo and Dominic Cook, Sebastian Creswell, and a couple servers, Sandra Vasquez and Erica Swanson. They're currently running a rotating schedule. One of our guys got in and got a shot of the schedule for last night," she said, putting it on the screen. "Riccardo, Dominic, and Sandra were the ones on around the time of the kidnapping."

"Please tell me you're more than just narrowing things down for me?" Seth sighed. "Please tell me you have more than who *didn't* do it?"

She shook her head. "Not at this time."

"Fine. Keep looking."

"Trust me, sir, we're doing our best. I've been cross-referencing between the Rossi's, and Jillian's and Aaron's cases to find connections."

"Wait a minute. Have you looked into the Rodchenko family? They may have wanted Katie for leverage," Seth pointed out.

"We're working that angle at the moment, sir," she confirmed. "What has Nick found out from his end?"

"Um, actually, Director Shaw, if I could have a moment with you?" Seth asked, knowing this would be a difficult conversation.

When they were in the hallway, Director Shaw crossed his arms as he leaned against the wall. "Make it snappy, Simmons. We have an investigation to get back to."

"Sir, I'm afraid we have a mole."

*   *   *

Katie woke up several hours later with a clearer head. "This must be what Frosty feels like," she said and shuddered from the cold before she sneezed.

Hearing a plate slide on a wooden tray toward her right, she turned to see a tray of food on the bed next to her. Taking inventory of all sounds around the room, she poked her toe out from under the blanket and used it to pull the tray close enough to reach, when she felt comfortable that she was alone.

She dove into the sandwich, keeping a watchful eye out for any movement. Afterward, she broke open the bag of chips, and downed the can of soda. That's when she saw the note on the tray. She picked it up with shaking hands and opened it. It read:

Dearest Katie,

Thank you for joining me for dinner. When we build a closer relationship of trust, you can indulge in the art supplies I have provided. I will make myself known to you when the time is right. Until then, know that I have admired you for quite some time.

Fondest wishes, your admirer

Katie didn't know what to do, so she tucked it under the pillow provided for her before she pushed the tray away. She would play her capture's game. She endured her father's abuse until she could escape. She would endure this as well.

While the morning sun provided the much needed light, what it revealed sent a shudder down her spine. She noted the shrine across the room, and just about threw up when she saw her scarf with Aaron's bloody handprint on it. She also saw more of the collage of photos that coated the walls. Whoever this was, had been watching her from her first day of school. They were only pictures of her, though. Her face stared at her from every corner of the room.

On the wall with the shrine, there were articles from the newspapers of the attacks, along with Jillian's and Aaron's obituaries. Marked across their obituaries in red marker was the word, '*Mistake*.' He wanted to make it clear to her that their deaths were unintentional.

"I don't care if it was unintentional. They're gone and it's your fault!" Katie shouted. She jumped when she heard a stomp on the floor above. Cowering in fear against the bed post, she waited to see if someone came downstairs, but they never did.

* * *

When Seb walked into the café that morning around eleven, Dom called him into the kitchen. "Have you seen the news this morning?"

"Nope. What's up?" he asked, clocking in.

"Katie's missing."

As soon as he said that, Seb froze. He gulped and took a couple deep breaths to slow his spinning head. With his hand visibly shaking, he replaced the timecard in its holder and turned to Dominic. "What did you say?"

"Katie's been missing since last night. The news has a video of a truck plastered all across it asking for any information."

Seb braced himself on the metal table and took a couple more deep breaths. His worst fears had come to fruition. "Are you telling me Katie was taken from the campus?"

Riccardo walked out of the office, into a strange scene. "Are you okay, Seb? You look as if you're going to pass out," he said, helping him to a chair. "You're shaking like a leaf. What happened?"

"Katie's missing. He didn't know," Dom said, looking as if he was doing his best to hold it together himself. "I saw it on the news this morning."

"*What?*"

"Go look it up online."

Riccardo quickly went to the office with Dom and Seb behind him. They watched the video in shock.

"Who did it?" Seb demanded.

"The FBI and police are working on it." Dom pointed out, "It says to click on that link for live updates."

Riccardo clicked the link. With not a lot to go on, the police and FBI were pleading with the citizens of Cleveland for any tips. Some were coming in from those in the garage, but that was all they could see.

"I need to call Ethan." Seb picked up his phone with his hands trembling. Turning it on for the first time that morning, he was shocked to find several text and voicemail messages from Ethan.

*   *   *

"My word! Where have you been?" Ethan demanded, answering his phone.

"Who is it?" Nick asked.

"Seb. Finally," Ethan sighed, and then turned his attention back to the phone. "Seriously, dude! Don't you turn your phone on?"

"Not on my day off. What's going on? Where's Katie?"

"She's missing."

"Got that much from the news. Who do you think did it? Do you think it was the Rossi's?"

"No. That's where I've been all night and today."

"You're at Giovanni's?" Seb asked in shock. Both owners looked at him in surprise.

"Yes. Nick's here too. We've all been looking. The Rossi's have even sent out their men to scour the city, with not a lot of luck. We're slowly narrowing the list, though."

"Any suspects?"

"Not at the moment."

"Do you want me to come over?"

"No, man, you can't do anything. We really can't do anything either, but keep an eye on what's going on."

"Please keep me updated?"

"Keep your phone on…even on your day off," Ethan snapped.

"Have you told the others?" Seb asked. Feeling guilty for the date he was on the night before, and the fact that he left the girl's apartment just in time to make it to work, while Katie was missing all night.

"Yeah. I didn't want them seeing it on the television or reading it online."

"Wonder what her dad thinks?"

"Don't know. Don't care. He hasn't shown up here yet. I have to agree with Katie's sentiment in this. She and I have talked, and I personally don't care for the man."

"What about Stacey? Has anyone called her?"

"You can. Not sure what can be done. It's my understanding her uncle is a higher-up FBI agent in Washington DC, so she probably knows already. Look, they already have quite a jump on us. I only hope it's not so much that we can't find her."

"I *do not* want to bury another friend," Seb said, tears of anger and hurt stinging his eyes. "Tell me what I can do."

"Honestly, nothing. Trust me, it's being done on all fronts. Giovanni's been chasing after his guys. You should see him. He's taken control of things from this end. Also, his dad has some connection into the police and FBI, and is getting fed information from them as it comes in."

"Wow," he whistled. "That's kind of scary."

"It is, but if it finds Katie, I'm not going to complain."

"Me neither."

"I'll keep you posted."

"Thanks."

*   *   *

Katie's lawyer, Jim Anderson, her dad (Brent), and the Sherriff from West Springs, Oklahoma stood in front of reporters. "We are getting hourly updates from the authorities in Cleveland and have no further information at this time," the Sherriff said near the end of his statement. "Thank you for your prayers and support."

"Please," Brent pleaded into the microphone. "Please release my Katie and return her. She is an innocent. If anyone has any information, please call the Cleveland FBI or police."

Jim pulled him away from the microphone before anything else was said, while Officer Herman Williams stood on the sidelines for crowd control with a broken heart. He remembered her from the accident and prayed for her swift return and that she would not be hurt. He knew what she had been through growing up and only wanted the best for her.

The town had her face plastered all over the social media with pleas for information. Ty, Eden, Emily, Ryan, Eric, and Serenity used every outlet they could think of from Oklahoma. Knowing ultimately God was the One in control, Eric and Serenity also set up a continuous prayer vigil at the church. As people had time, they would come down to the church to pray. When they were not there, they still promised to pray at work.

*   *   *

Katie woke up praying. She knew her best chance of survival or rescue was going to come from God. As she prayed, she remembered the verse, Isaiah 41:10, which says, "*So do not fear, for I am with you; do not be dismayed, for I am your God. I will strengthen you and help you; I will uphold you with my righteous right hand.*"

"Thank you," Katie whispered, wiping away the tears that streaked her face. She took a staggered breath and said aloud, "I know You love me and will take care of me. I have struggled for so long to trust You, but I think deep down I have been trusting You all along. However this turns out, I want You to know when I gave You a challenge, You more than proved it. Anything else was my own fault. I ask You, Father, to be my Father. I ask You, Jesus, to be my Savior. I ask You, Spirit, to be my guide. Whether these are my last minutes on earth or not, I want to have the confidence of knowing whatever I go through, that when it is over, I can run into Your arms. Please forgive me for my sins, with pride and anger at the top of those lists. I ask that whatever time I have left, You make my life count in some way. Please allow me the honor of knowing I did something for Your Kingdom here on Earth."

Jeremiah 29:11, came to her mind, *"For I know the plans I have for you,"* declares the LORD, *"plans to prosper you and not to harm you, plans to give you hope and a future."*

"I know, Father. You have given me a hope and a future with You. I will hold onto that…whatever happens. You are mine and I am Yours. I can never repay You enough for that gift and only ask You to forgive me and allow me to be Your child. In Jesus' most precious name I pray, Amen," she said, and sighed.

By the amount of light coming into the windows, she guessed it to be close to sunset. By that point, she figured out she was in a basement. And by the looks of the spider nests all over and mouse feces in the corners, it wasn't well-kept at all. She shuddered at the spider nests. She couldn't stand spiders, and in the position she was in, she wouldn't be able to kill them either.

She woke with a headache and hoped it would stop soon. That's when she sneezed and felt it through her entire body. "Oh just great," she whispered. "Now I catch a cold on top of it?" She shivered. "Fine. Whatever happens, I promise to trust You, Lord."

*   *   *

Nick walked down to the kitchen for a snack, when he stopped in his tracks. He heard Marcus, the chef, speaking Russian into his phone quietly in the corner of the kitchen. Knowing Russian as one of his languages, he caught the words 'girl,' 'kidnapped,' and 'Giovanni's in charge' out of the conversation before he stormed the kitchen.

Slamming Marcus against the wall, he got into his face, and demanded, "Mind telling me who you were talking to, mate?"

Ethan heard the commotion and ran to get Joey, since Giovanni was busy with the investigation and his father.

"I-I don't know what you are talking about," Marcus stammered.

"Let me try this again," he said and put him further up the wall before he slammed him again, "*Who* were you talking to?"

"What's going on?" Joey asked. "Please unhand our chef."

Nick shook his head. "Nope, sorry, mate. And, I don't think you want me to."

"Why not?"

"Redial his phone."

Joey scooped Marcus' phone off the ground and redialed. "Who is this?" Joey challenged, when someone answered the phone with a Russian greeting. Instead of answering, the person hung up the phone and didn't answer when he called them back again. Joey then scanned the text messages, getting angrier with each one. Looking toward Marcus, he demanded, "Who are you?"

"I am Marcus, your chef," he said, nervously glancing from the phone, to Joey, to Nick. "I have been your chef for seven years. You know who I am."

"Dad!" Joey shouted as loud as he could. "Dad, bring Giovanni and get in here!"

The scene Lucca, Giovanni, and two of their guys walked into shocked them. "What in heaven's name is going on here?" Lucca demanded.

"No one's penetrated this family in over forty years, huh?" Joey challenged.

"Yes. I take pride in that."

"May want to rethink that statement."

"Why does Nick have Marcus against the wall?" Giovanni asked.

"Because if he didn't, I would have him flat out on the ground," Joey said, handing the phone to Giovanni.

Lucca looked over his shoulder, while Giovanni scanned the text messages, getting more agitated with each one. He glared at Marcus as he ordered, "Sal, Dante, take Marcus downstairs and get him ready for questioning."

"Wait. What?" Nick asked, as Sal pulled him off Marcus. "What are you doing?"

"He works for the Rodchenko Family," Giovanni explained. "First off, he is now a traitor to our family. Secondly, he may have information on Katie."

"Are you going to hurt him?" Ethan asked, horrified.

"I will do what it takes to find her," Giovanni said, sternly.

"She wouldn't want that." Nick shook his head. "Take him downstairs and cut the line of communication, fine, but don't hurt him. He could still prove useful."

Giovanni narrowed his eyes at Nick. "How?"

"If he is from this family you are saying he's from, he may have information. If you hurt him or worse yet, kill him, he won't be able to give you any."

"I see. Sal, Dante, take him down and find out what he knows about Katie. After that, let him sit there and rot," Giovanni instructed.

"Yes, sir," they said, and took Marcus down the staircase to the basement, with him yelling and screaming the entire way down.

"Very good, son. You will make a wonderful leader. I am very proud of you," Lucca said with pride, and left the kitchen.

"Me too, bro. I didn't think you had it in you, but you do," Joey congratulated him before he followed his dad out of the kitchen.

Ethan left with them, visibly shaken up by the scene. He was not sure what would happen, but he decided the less he knew the better.

When the kitchen was empty, Nick looked at Giovanni and said, "You don't want to do this, man."

"Do what?"

"Lead this family. This isn't you. Katie knows it and so do I. Do you really want to be responsible for people dying? You want your father to be proud of you for being a criminal?"

"He's not…what do you mean?"

"Both he and Joey said they were proud of the way you stepped up, because they didn't think you had it in you. You almost sent Marcus down there to get beaten to death."

"To help Katie."

"What would she do if she found out that's how you found her?"

He went to say something, but stopped and shoved his hands into his pockets. "She would be ticked."

"Beyond measure. Do you really want to do this?"

He looked up at Nick, hoping he would understand. "I don't have a choice."

"Yes, you do. It's going to be up to you."

"What do you mean?"

"Keep it between us?"

"I promise."

Nick leaned in and whispered, "I could get killed for telling you this, and I understand that, but you are important to both me and Katie, so I am telling you that I am FBI."

Giovanni took a step back, stunned. "*What?*"

"Katie's not, but I am. Look, if you don't want to do this for the rest of your life, I can get you out."

Giovanni looked toward both staircases to make sure no one was listening, while he debated in his head for several moments. *This was his chance. Could he really leave the family? He didn't want to lead them. Yes, he liked that the men looked up to him, but he knew what else his father did.* He leaned into Nick and asked, "How?"

"When this is over, find me and we'll talk. I can get you out of here, but right now Katie has the utmost importance. In the meantime, don't do anything I can arrest you for. Am I making myself clear?"

"Yes, sir."

"One more question?"

"Yeah?"

"Do you know who the spy is in the agency? The information you got only could have come from inside the FBI."

"Yes, sir."

Nick looked at him and sternly said, "Tell no one. I will get you out."

"Deal," Giovanni said, shaking Nick's hand, feeling like a weight was lifted off his shoulders. He knew at that point he would find Katie, and afterward, he would be free of his father. He would be able to chase his dreams after all.

*   *   *

"Aaron took the last moments of his life to write the letter 'C' in his own blood," Seth said, thinking aloud. "Have all of the Cook's Corner Café's crew alibis been verified?"

"What do you mean?" Claire asked. "According to the schedule, Riccardo, Dominic, and Sandra were working. The others have been tracked via cameras to find their whereabouts."

"Sebastian Creswell is verified?" Dakota asked.

"Yes. He was in the food court with a girl," she said, clicking away on her computer until she brought up the photo with a time stamp on the screen.

"What about the three who worked? Were they there the entire time?" Dakota questioned.

Claire shook her head. "I don't think that's possible *to* verify."

Emma looked up in surprise. "Do me a favor. How far back does that wonder computer of yours work?"

"I can see the wheels turning from here. What are you thinking?" Seth asked Emma.

"I want her to look up the location of both Dominic and Riccardo, if she can, and see if she can calculate where both of them were for all of the attacks."

Claire furrowed her brow. "Why?"

Emma got up and went over to the dry erase board containing the photos of the girls. "The café is about a block from Katie's dorm. All of the girls have similar features to Katie. Katie only frequented one of three places on a regular basis – the bookstore, the grocery store, and the café. Nine out of ten times, the victim knows their assailant. What if the other girls were a dry run or a mark of frustration that he couldn't have Katie because she was with Jillian? In essence, she was protected by Director Shaw. Now, in looking at these, the attacks were closer in proximity to her dorm each time. What if Jillian, being bundled due to the winter weather, resembled Katie a bit too much? What if Aaron, bundled and wearing Katie's hat and scarf looked like Katie, and when he realized it wasn't Katie, and that it was a guy, that he panicked. What if, when Aaron realized who he was, tried to kill him, and in turn it was a survival of the strongest? If that's the case, both Dominic and Riccardo are two big, muscular, Italian guys. Could one of them overpower Aaron enough to kill him?"

"Are you saying the attacker thought Jillian and Aaron were Katie?" Director Shaw asked.

"What if?" Emma asked. "That, along with the fact that their last name starts with the letter 'C.' That could be what Aaron was trying to tell us. What if the 'C' stands for Cook and/or café? He was dying. He didn't have much time to think."

Seth turned to Claire and ordered, "Find out where both men were. We know a woman didn't attack them. That only leaves the two guys on shift that night. Find out where Dominic and Riccardo were."

"Yes, sir," she said, and typed as quickly as her fingers would move.

*   *   *

"Thank you," Lucca said and hung up. He looked at Andre and said, "Go tell Sal and Dante to leave Marcus alone. We need to find out where Dominic and Riccardo Cook were last night."

"*What*?" Ethan, Nick, and Giovanni all three asked, taken aback by the turn of events.

"Call Seb and find out where Riccardo and Dominic were," he ordered Giovanni. "Do it discretely. We don't want to tip any hands."

"What's going on?" he asked, dialing from Ethan's phone, since Seb's number was already programmed into it.

"The investigation has shifted."

*   *   *

"Hey, Ethan," Seb answered the phone.

"Hi, Seb, it's Giovanni. Ethan's here, but I need to ask you something."

"Sure."

"Can you step outside so no one will overhear?"

"Sure. Give me a minute. Hey, Dom!" He called to him. "I'm going to take a few minute break."

"Go head," he called back.

When Seb was outside, he asked, "What's going on?"

"I need you to find out where Dominic and Riccardo were last night."

"That's easy. I make the schedule. They were here. Sandra was waitress."

"Are you positive they were there the entire time?"

"I can't answer that for sure. I was off last night. Why?"

"Because they seem to be our latest leads."

"I don't think they would hurt her."

"Don't think or do you know that for sure?"

Seb gulped as his heart skipped a beat. *Could one of the men he worked for hurt Katie? Or worse yet, could they have killed Jillian and Aaron?* "I don't know," he admitted.

"Act like nothing happened. Pretend you still don't know anything."

"Okay," he agreed.

"Thank you," he said, and hung up. Giovanni turned to his father and said, "Pursue that angle. Seb can't be one hundred percent sure. Both men were working last night, which would give them access to the dorm within a block. They also would have known when Katie left the café."

"Working on it already," Lucca confirmed. "We'll find her, Giovanni. I have given you my word, and you know I don't go back on it."

"That I do," he said, and then glanced at Nick, who nodded in response.

*   *   *

Listening to Seb's conversation, he realized he was now a suspect. He had to get out of there and get to Katie. Making up an excuse that he needed to go get something for the diner, he left, making a bee-line for Katie.

*   *   *

To Katie, time seemed to crawl. She sneezed for what seemed like the hundredth time for her, followed by a cough and sniffle. She kept an eye out for some sign of her captor, but saw none.

Pulling on her handcuffs to the point that her wrists were bleeding, she couldn't loosen them no matter how hard she tried. She pulled and yanked, hoping to make enough noise to alert someone she was up, but nothing happened. The house was completely silent. The silence was almost deafening.

That's when she heard the door open upstairs. A single set of footsteps cleared the floor above her. Hearing the footsteps as the person went into a room, she heard the slamming of dresser drawers, along with closet doors. Finally, the door opened at the top of the staircase, and with each step taken on the staircase, Katie's heart rate picked up speed. She thought for a moment that her heart was going to explode in fear as Dominic stepped into the light of the basement. Petrified, she couldn't form a single word or thought.

"Hello, my dear," he said, with a bag of food from the restaurant in his hands, along with a cup of liquid. Placing the gym bag on the floor that he brought down, he explained, "I brought your favorite, fresh-squeezed lemonade, fried chicken, and mashed potatoes." He quickly cleared the space between the stairs and the bed she was attached to, and sat on the side of the bed. "Are you hungry?"

She sneezed in response. Wiping her nose with her sleeve, she squeaked out, "What am I doing here? What are you doing?"

"I have been in love with you since you first walked into the café with that friend of yours from Oklahoma. I missed you so much during the breaks when you went home with Jillian, I couldn't take it."

"*So you raped women?*" Katie shrieked. "What about Jill? What about Aaron? What are you going to do with me?"

"I am honestly sorry about Jill and Aaron. I knew you would be staying around for Christmas Break, and I wanted to take care of you. I thought Jillian was you."

"You *killed* her!"

"It was an accident. I need you to understand I thought she was you. I tried to grab her, but she hurt me and made me angry."

"You were trying to take her! Of course she fought back. What about Aaron? Why did you kill him?"

Anger flashed across his face as he remembered the attack. "I had no choice. He was going to kill me if I didn't kill him first."

Katie took a deep breath. She understood agitating him would not help the situation, so she shifted her strategy. "Look, I appreciate your admiration, but this is not the way to show it. If you wanted to spend Christmas with me, why didn't you just ask?"

"You would never go out with me."

Was he serious? Of course she wouldn't go out with him! She bit her tongue to stop the words she wanted to shout at him. "Dom, I like you as a friend. I'm getting sick in here, though. It's too cold for me. I need heat. If you want to take care of me, wouldn't it be better to take me upstairs where it's warm?"

"Upstairs? Like to my bedroom?" he asked, hopeful.

Katie cringed. "I, uh, am saving myself for marriage."

"We could get married," he said, brushing his hand on her cheek. "I know everything about you. I know we would make a perfect couple."

"I think –"

"I even have a tablet set up on an easel for you in my spare room, with a variety of art supplies. You can draw to your heart's content," he said, pleased with himself. "I love your drawings. See, I even have some on my wall. Look," he went over to one on the wall, "I won it at the auction your class did for charity. I paid the most so I could have it on my wall."

"I see that. I appreciate it."

He ran over and forcefully cupped her face with his hands. "You are so beautiful! I can't wait to have you. Look," he ran over to the corner of the room, to a mannequin covered with a sheet. He uncovered it to reveal a gorgeous wedding dress. "You will look stunning in this!"

Katie's body trembled in fear. Dominic had literally lost his mind. "Dom, please let me go?" she asked, as a tear slowly crawled down her cheek. "I –"

"I need you," he said, returning to the bedside. In desperation, he pleaded with her to understand, "I love you. Don't you get that?"

Katie didn't answer. She was petrified beyond words. She had never run across anyone like this before. Looking toward heaven, she said to God, "I trust You. This is all up to You how it ends."

"Oh! Thank you!" Dominic said and grabbed her, hugging her. He leaned down and kissed her neck. "I know we will make a wonderful couple!"

Katie wiggled to get loose. Losing her composure, she broke down in tears.

He backed away and asked, "Are those happy tears?"

Katie shook her head in response, unable to verbally say a word. She took a deep breath, resigning herself to do whatever she needed to do to gain his trust, in order to plan her moment of escape.

"Are you happy?"

"Honestly? I'm too cold and hungry."

"Oh, here you go. Here, let me feed you, my darling," he said and opened the food he brought for her.

As he slowly fed her each bite, she had to force herself to swallow. She wasn't sure if she truly hated him or felt bad for him. He seemed so pleased with himself for knowing everything she liked.

"How long are you going to hold me here? I'm getting sick," she said, and sneezed again.

When she wiped her nose on her sweater, he commented, "I don't want you getting any sicker. I will take care of you. You won't have to want for anything. What if we take a trip? You know, just the two of us…to somewhere warm?"

"Dom –"

"I love how you say my name," he said, cutting her off. He rested his hand on the side of her face, as he continued, "I adore your smile, and love to hear your voice."

"Dom, you have to let me go. This isn't right."

"Of course it's right. What colors do you want? What theme are you thinking?"

"For what?"

"Our wedding? How do you want it?"

She lost it. "I don't!"

"Yes, you do."

"No, I don't!" She tugged on her handcuffs. "I *want* out of here! I want Nick and Giovanni! I want Ethan and Seb. What I don't want is *you*!"

"Yes, you do. I know you do. You always smile at me. You talk to me all the time and are happy to see me. I know you love me like I love you."

"No, I don't. Let-me-go!" she screamed, yanking and pulling on the cuffs until her wrists bled again. They were raw at best.

"Oh, stop. You're hurting yourself. Here, I'll take care of you."

"Don't touch me!" she shrieked and kicked with her feet. "Leave me alone!"

He fought through her legs and grabbed her face, firmly holding her chin. She froze, staring at him in horror. "You have to quiet down or the neighbors will hear you."

"Leave-me-alone!" Katie shouted again.

He covered her mouth and got in her face. "You will regret it if you scream again. Do we have an understanding?" She nodded in response, so he removed his hand. "There, much better, don't you think?" he asked, hopeful for her cooperation.

She shook her head, beside herself.

He sighed, as he rested his hand on the side of her face. "You're beautiful and so full of life. I want to bottle that. I want to feel that every day and hold it close to me. I want to hold *you* close to me. Here, let me warm you," he said and slid up next to her.

Her body trembled in fear as he wrapped his arms around her. "Please, not now. I-I need my blanket," she pleaded.

"Yes, the blanket is a good idea." He wrapped the blanket around both of them. Resting his head on her shoulder from behind, he inched closer. After a minute, he ran his hand up her thigh toward her waist.

"Stop. Please?" Katie begged. "Go away."

"So, you don't want to go with me?"

"Of course not!" she shrieked, panicking again. If she went to another state or worse yet, another country, there is no way she would ever be found. "I want you to leave me alone. I don't want you touching me. I wouldn't marry you if you were the last man on Earth! I will never voluntarily go with you anywhere. You are a sadistic psychopath!"

He stood and slapped her. When he did, her head hit the bars of the bed, spinning her head out of control. She shook it to clear her mind as he got in her face. "All I wanted to do was take care of you and love you. Your yelling abusive words toward me show me that you don't want that."

"Not a chance," she snapped as the green flashed through her eyes.

"You know you're going to freeze to death before anyone ever finds you. In the meantime, I'm going to go hop on a plane for the Bahamas. Enjoy your time," he snarled. "I want you to think of how much better we could have been together."

"I would never be with you. I can't believe you would ever think that. You have blood on your hands. And worse yet, they were my friends. God will judge your heart, and may He have mercy on your soul!"

"Venomous, little witch!" He growled, grabbing her throat.

She kicked and squirmed, struggling to get free as her head felt like it would explode from the pressure. She couldn't get any air. Her pulse pounded in her head. She was sure these were her last minutes. '*I love You, Lord,*' she said in her head before she went unconscious.

When her body slumped over on the bed, Dom stepped back, horrified at what he had done. He knew the authorities were closing in. With the winter weather keeping the temperatures at twenty degrees and a wind chill factor of nine, he flipped open the windows before he left. If she did gain consciousness, she would freeze to death before anyone would get to her. In the meantime, he would have the time he would need to escape.

*   *   *

"Well, this is interesting," Claire said, staring at her computer.

"What is?" Seth asked.

"Well, according to what I could pull from the campus cameras on the nights of all of the attacks, it seems that both men were working."

"Bring them both in for questioning," Director Shaw ordered. "In the meantime, get a search warrant. Get a list of their addresses for the times in question and any vehicles or property they may have rented or owned at that time."

"Done," Claire said, printing off a list and handing it to Seth as he, Dakota, and Todd ran out of the office.

"Good job, Brenner. I knew we picked a good one in you," Director Shaw said, patting her shoulder before he left the office. Over his shoulder, he said, "Let me know when they bring them in."

"Yes, sir."

*   *   *

Katie slowly opened her eyes, her head pounding beyond belief. Focusing her eyes on an object floating in the air, it took her a moment to realize it was a snow flake. To her horror, Dominic had left the windows open in the basement before he left. She had no idea how much time had passed. All she knew was that her fingers and toes were red from the cold and that her body could not stop shivering. Jeremiah 29:11 came to her mind again, so she began to recite it. Knowing hypothermia was close to setting in, she wanted to stay conscious. *"For I know the plans I have for you,"* declares the LORD, *"plans to prosper you and not to harm you, plans to give you hope and a future,"* she repeated over and over again.

That's when she heard the door upstairs get kicked in and she jumped. Shouting and yelling commenced as a crowd of footsteps flooded into the house. She continued to recite the verse with a renewed excitement, " *'For I know the plans I have for you,"* declares the LORD, *"plans to prosper you and not to harm you, plans to give you hope and a future.' 'For I know the plans I have for you,"* declares the LORD, *"plans to prosper you and not to harm you, plans to give you hope and a future.' 'For I know the plans I have for you,"* declares the LORD, *"plans to prosper you and not to harm you, plans to give you hope and a future.'"*

"Clear in here!" she heard various people shout as the group cleared the house.

"Door," she heard before the door at the top of the stairs was kicked in and a rush of agents flooded the basement.

"Katie!" Dakota looked at her, stunned. He scooped the blanket from off the ground on his way to the bed. He took his warm coat off and wrapped her in it before he wrapped the blanket around her as well.

Todd took his coat off and wrapped her feet. "What's she saying?" he asked.

"Dunno." He shrugged. He leaned in and repeated, "Declares the Lord, "Plans to prosper"…I'm not a hundred percent sure what she's saying. It's something about hope."

"Is it, *'For I know the plans I have for you,"* declares the LORD, *"plans to prosper you and not to harm you, plans to give you hope and a future? "'* one of the other agents asked.

Dakota listened again as she continuously recited it over and over. "Yeah. What's she saying, Fredrickson?"

The agent knelt in front of her and asked, "Katie, are you saying Jeremiah 29:11?"

She nodded as she continued to recite the verse under her breath.

"I'm thinking she's repeating the verse to keep herself focused. As cold as she is, hypothermia would be a concern. Is the ambulance almost here?"

"Yes," Seth confirmed, coming into the basement. "They're about three minutes out."

The agent brushed Katie's hair off her face, as Todd released her hands from the handcuffs. "Katie," he said gently, in order to keep her calm as she rocked in place, "the ambulance is on the way. They'll be here shortly. You're safe. God has protected you and you are safe. Do you hear me?"

She nodded, but continued to recite the verse over and over again.

While they waited for the ambulance, Seth, for the first time, took note of all the pictures on the walls and shook his head. "It takes all kinds."

"We got you and you're safe. Katie, can you understand me?" Dakota asked. She only nodded in response as she recited the verse under her breath. "Nick's taking care of something. He wanted to be here to get you, but he has something very important he needs to take care of first. He'll be at the hospital later. Do you understand?"

She again only nodded in response as she continued to recite the verse.

"She's gone, man," Todd shook his head as he crossed his arms, heartbroken. "I think that God of hers will be the only One who can help her now."

*   *   *

"They found her," Lucca confirmed over the phone approximately three hours after they changed the direction of their investigation toward the Cook brothers. Cheers were heard throughout the house. "They're taking her to University Hospital."

"If you don't mind, I would like to go with Nick to the hospital?" Giovanni asked his dad.

"Of course, son. Keep in contact. I will handle the issue downstairs."

"Leave him for now. Let him sweat for a bit," Giovanni said, doing his best to follow what Nick said about not doing anything he could arrest him for. "I'll take care of it later."

"If you could drop me at the café, Seb and I will meet you guys at the hospital?" Ethan asked.

"Sure. C'mon," Nick agreed.

After they dropped Ethan off, Giovanni turned to Nick and said, "I know you want to get to Katie, so do I, but I don't want anything else to happen and chance me chickening out on this."

"On what?"

"You want my dad, along with the police and FBI moles? I can give them to you. How are you going to help me?"

"We'll protect you until you can testify at their trials. Then afterward, we'll give you a new start, a fresh start. You can do anything you want."

"I want to follow my dreams."

"That's all Katie wants for you, too."

"Then, let's do this."

"If that's what you want," Nick said, and turned his vehicle toward the FBI office. He called Director Shaw on the way in to prepare him, and got an update on Katie while he was on the phone. "She's in shock and is suffering from hypothermia. From what they can tell, though, he didn't rape her."

"Good," Giovanni said, relieved. "Who was it?"

"She was found in Dominic's basement."

He sat back in his seat, stunned. "Wow! Wasn't expecting that one."

"No one was."

*   *   *

"How is she?" Nick asked one of the two agents guarding the door when he finally arrived at the hospital several hours later. He had to get all of the information from Giovanni and get him settled in a safe house before he could go to her.

"When they brought her in, she was reciting some verse. They gave her a mild sedative because she was such a mess when she came in, but are watching her very closely due to the hypothermia. They also started IVs with warm fluid to increase her body temperature, and get it under control. She's in shock, man. I don't know what she'll be like when she wakes up. You should have seen that basement." He shook his head. "It was twisted. There were photos of her all over, along with a wedding dress. They also found the scarf with Aaron's bloody handprint and the earrings. I can't imagine what all she went through."

Nick huffed. "Any good news?"

"The doctor said outside of that and the mental trauma, he didn't rape her. He did try to strangle her, though."

"I see. Thank you."

"You may be able to get something out of her. No one else has been able to. When she is awake, all she does is recite some verse."

He nodded before he went into the room. Catching his breath when he saw her, he was shocked to see her face looking sunken. She lacked the life he was used to seeing in her. When she looked up at him, he said, "Morning, sunshine." The tears instantly flowed from her eyes as he went over to her bedside, "Ohhhh, hey, hey, it's okay. You're safe," he said, holding her. She cried on his shoulder for several minutes before he rested one of his hands on the side of her face. Using his thumb, he wiped her tears away. "I'm sorry I wasn't here sooner. I had to take care of something." She gave him a questioning look, so he explained, "I had to help Giovanni achieve his dreams. He flipped, and while he was at it named the moles in the agency and the police departments."

She furrowed her brow.

"There was a mole in the FBI as well as a couple of police officers who were feeding Lucca information. This enabled him to stay a step ahead of us. Giovanni knew who they were. We're going to protect him in a safe house until all the trials are over. Once they're over, he's going to go into the witness protection program where he can follow his dream."

Katie nodded in response.

"Do you know what that is? He said when you first found out you laughed."

She nodded again.

"What is it? What does he want to do?"

She shook her head.

"I really want to hear your voice. Please talk to me."

Shuddering, she began to rock in her seated position.

"You're breaking my heart, Katie." Nick held her as he prayed that God would show her she was safe and would reach her heart. It was tucked away in a place only God could get to.

* * *

After picking at her food for two days, and Nick pushing the fluids, she woke up a couple days after she was rescued with a clearer head. Reaching over, she ran her fingers through Nick's hair while he slept with his head on the bed.

"Katie?" he asked. She nodded. "Katie, I would really like to hear your voice. You haven't said a word for over two days. Please talk to me?" he begged. He had been trying to get her to talk for a couple days without any success.

She took a deep breath before she asked, "Dominic?"

He frowned. "We don't know where he is.

Looking toward the ceiling to stop herself from crying, she shook her head, upset. "He said the Bahamas."

"We'll keep an eye out for him, but that's not a lot to go on. Pretty sure he wouldn't tell you exactly where he was going, but we'll look into it," he said, knowing they already tracked him going into Canada before they lost him.

"I'm scared."

"I know. Look, what you did in the last month, is something we have not been able to do in years. You helped not only shut the Rossi family down, but you gave Giovanni his freedom. He'll be safe and be free now for the rest of his life thanks to you."

"What about Lucca and Joey?"

"Lucca's in jail, and won't be getting out for quite some time. Trust me, Director Shaw is pushing the DA hard on this one. And, Joey didn't do anything that we can prove, so he's free."

"You know Jillian and Aaron were killed and those girls were raped because of me?"

"What? No. That wasn't because of you."

"He wanted me." She sighed. "I wish he would have taken me from the beginning, because then both Aaron and Jillian would still be here…and be together."

"Don't say that. You can't control what he did. One thing you will learn in working at the FBI, is that there are some twisted people out there. It's our job to catch them. We not only have to catch them, but we also need to do it with enough evidence that they won't get back out."

"I understand that," she took a deep breath to control her emotions, "but in this case, he even admitted Jillian's and Aaron's death were accidents. He said he thought Jillian was me. If I would have went to the dorm first, Jillian would still be alive. He also said that Aaron's death was in self-defense. He said he thought he was me and once he realized he wasn't,

Aaron was too angry. He said if he didn't kill him, that Aaron would have killed him."

"Katie," he took her hands into his and rubbed them as he said, "we're not in control of this world – that's God's job. There's one thing you need to understand though, that's the concept of free will."

"What do you mean?"

"God doesn't sit up there and treat us like puppets. He wants us to love Him and serve Him of our own free will."

"I get that."

"What you may not understand is that free will has a dark side. He has given people the free will to do what they want. Sometimes this is a good thing, sometimes it's not. Do I wish He would stop evil? Oh yeah! Do I wish He would wipe out evil thoughts and ideas? Yep. Do I wish this was a utopia of some sort? Actually, no. You see, with free will comes responsibility. Some people take that and do twisted things, like Dominic. We don't know why. We don't understand it. We don't know why it happens or even sometimes how to deal with it. That's where God's love and guidance comes into play. When we're one of His, we have a place to go when we can't process what's going on around us. I don't know if this makes sense or not, but it's how it works."

"Actually, it does," she agreed. "When I was in that basement, I made a decision. Even though I was scared out of my mind, I wanted to know that whatever happened, I would be with God in the end."

"Are you saying what I think you're saying?"

"Remember the challenge I gave to God at the beginning of break?"

"Yes," his heart skipped a beat in excitement, "do you have a verdict yet?"

"Yes."

"And?"

"I was guilty, and He forgave my sins."

"Wonderful!" he said and hugged her.

"There's more," she said, pulling away so she could see his face. "While I prayed, the Lord continued to put verses in my head to comfort me."

"I heard that. I also heard one was Jeremiah 29:11."

"Yes. That verse kept me conscious and I know without God I wouldn't have made it."

"That's music to my ears."

Stacey lightly knocked on the door as she and Scott walked in. "Morning."

"Hi," Katie greeted them. Her chest felt heavy, so her response lacked excitement.

Stacey sat down on the side of the bed as she said, "My uncle called to tell me where you were. Director Shaw is working with the DA, otherwise he would have been here before now. He also called me and asked me to come as well. There are quite a few people worried about you."

"I know."

"It's going to be a long walk, but I'm still willing to continue the journey with you."

"I would appreciate that. I know with God, you, Nick, and everyone else, that eventually I'll be okay. Right now, though, I'm struggling."

"That's understandable. It won't be easy, but it will be worth it. I understand your friend, Giovanni, will need you over the next few months as well."

"Do I get to see him?" she asked Nick.

"I'm sure I could arrange that, and he would appreciate it."

"What's going to happen to him?"

Nick hesitated giving too much information, and decided on, "He'll testify and then we'll take care of him."

"I see," Katie said in understanding.

"He'll be okay. I'll take care of him personally," Nick promised. "He has given up a lot and I want to help him achieve his dreams, and do it as a free man."

"Did he tell you what his dream was?"

"Not yet."

"He wants to be a veterinarian."

"Seriously?"

"I know. I told him he didn't seem like that type, but he said he loves animals."

"Got it."

Stacey cleared her throat as she looked toward Scott.

"Hey, man, I think the girls need to talk. Wanna go with me to get them something to eat? Pretty sure Katie would appreciate something other than hospital food," Scott pointed out.

"Sounds good." Nick squeezed Katie's hand before he left with Scott. "See ya in a bit."

"So," Stacey started, "I'm thinking we need to chat. You, my dear, have lost your spark. You have had a lot go on over the last month, so I'm going to sit back and you're going to let it all out."

"I don't know where to start."

"Start at the beginning."

Chapter 13

The Great Escape

A little over three hours after he left Katie, Dominic pulled up to the Canada border via the Rainbow Bridge in New York State. Guilt filled him to the point that he thought for sure there was still blood on his hands no matter how hard he scrubbed.

Choking Katie to the point that she went unconscious was something he never intended. He wanted her to love him. He saw the way she treated her friends and those she held close to her. The only thing he ever wanted was love and acceptance, but now he messed it up.

"Documents please," the border officer asked as Dominic pulled up for his turn. He scanned the passport, stamped it to Dominic's relief, and handed it back to him. "Enjoy your stay, Mr. Cook."

"Thank you," Dominic said, tucking his documents into the bag on the passenger's seat. He gave the border agent his real documents to see if his name had been sent out yet. He had a gun ready and within reach if he needed it, but to his surprise, it wasn't necessary.

As he passed into Ontario, Canada, he knew this would be a new beginning. He got through into Canada before they flagged his passport. Knowing it would set something off as soon as they notified the borders to be on the lookout for him, he would have to use the new identity he already had in his belongings in case of an emergency.

Would he be able to forget Katie, though? Would he be able to move on? She was all he could think about. He grabbed a couple of her photos before he left. They would have to be enough until he could see her again.

Song of Solomon 2: 11-12

For behold, the winter is past; the rain is over and gone. The flowers appear on the earth, the time of singing has come, and the voice of the turtledove is heard in our land.

Sneak Peek of Spring Shadows –

Grace Restored Series, Book 3

Spring Forward

Katie's rapid heartbeat was all she heard pounding in her ears while she scanned the area. Shadows danced around her, playing tricks with her eyes as a few strategically placed fluorescent bulbs lit what they could of the warehouse. Crates of various sizes were strewn about in uneven stacks, making navigation difficult. The musty warehouse smell, along with the scent of the wooden crates, overpowered Katie's senses while she continuously reminded herself to breathe with each step she took. *A warehouse? How original.* She shook her head.

The scuff of a shoe to her left made her jump. Silently, she crept around the wooden crate with her gun aimed and placed it on the back of the young man's head. "Police. Place your hands on your head. Otherwise don't move."

"Officer MacKenna, it's me, Damian. You know, Nick's friend?"

Katie let out a breath of relief. "Damian! What in Sam Hill are you doing here? You scared me to death!"

"I live here. Scary people work here, though, so I'm hiding."

Katie knelt beside him and asked, "Do you think you could get out of here safely? Is there a back way out?"

"I can get out the front unseen. What are you going to do, though? You can't stay in here. I've seen some nasty stuff over the last few months. These people will kill you on sight!"

"I'm not in here alone. There are three other officers in here with me."

"They have someone tied to a chair. I already called Nick. He's on his way."

"Where?"

"That way, on the other side of the warehouse," he said, pointing to his left. "He's got some vest on him with what looks like gray clay bars."

"Got it. I need you to get out there and tell Nick what's going on. Look," she placed her hands on his shoulders, crouching down to look at him at eye level, "I don't want anything to happen to you. You're only, what, eighteen years old?"

"I'm nineteen," he corrected.

"You have your whole life ahead of you. You're straightening out your life. Your GED should be in the mail any day. I want you to continue to chase after your dream."

"You're not all that old either. You shouldn't be in here."

Glancing around the warehouse, she explained, "I'm here because they're after me. I want to end this."

"You can't do it alone."

"I'm not alone. If I'm not done with what God has planned for me, He'll protect me."

"I hope you're right."

"I know I'm right," she said, confidently. "Now, go," she said, and then shoved him in the direction of the front of the warehouse.

Running outside, almost blinded by the amount of flashing lights from the federal, along with the police and rescue vehicles, Damian spotted Nick in the distance, talking with several people. Practically running to him, Damian hugged Nick, relief evident on his body.

"Wha...?" Nick was stunned for a moment before he saw the dirty face and grungy clothes of the young man he had been taking care of for several years. "Damian, what are you doing here?"

"She's here," he said, slightly panicked.

"Who?"

"Officer MacKenna! Katie! She's here. She's in the warehouse."

Looking toward the building Nick's stomach lurched. "Are you sure it was her?"

"Yes, I talked to her. She said – " A loud 'BOOM!' cut him off.

To Nick, everything suddenly began to move in slow motion. Damian's body slammed into his before Damian flew overhead, landing like a rag doll several feet away. Seeing his other friends and co-workers near him soar through the air, along with the debris from the warehouse, Nick curled into a ball under the car next to where he landed in order to prevent further damage. Covering his ears when glass shattered, metal twisted and turned, and screams and shouting joined the mix, creating a cannonade of thunderous disharmony. A deafening crash of vehicle that flipped and landed within feet of him sent a shockwave through his body that took his breath away. The ringing in his ears irritated him while he struggled to recover from the daze of surviving the devastation created around him. Looking toward the warehouse, he gulped when he remembered Katie was now encased in the mountainous remains. Adrenaline coursed through his body as he pushed to stand before staggering toward the warehouse – to Katie.

Seth grabbed him. "No, man, you can't go."

Dakota and Todd leapt in front of him to push him back as a secondary explosion went off toward the back of the warehouse. Hoping nothing else would explode, it took all three of them to hold Nick down.

"You can't go in there!" Seth shouted over the chaos.

"I have to get her! I can't leave her! I'm not losing her! Katie!" he shouted, struggling to get off the ground and get to the rubble that the warehouse had become. "KATIE! KATIE! NO!"

See the rest in Spring Shadows!

Books in the Grace Restored Series

Book 1   Book 2   Book 3

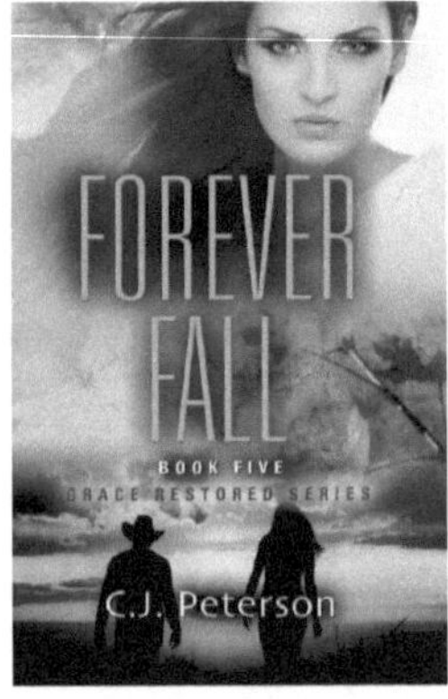

Book 4   Book 5

Also check out C.J. Peterson's other series –

The Holy Flame Trilogy

Divine Legacy Series

Connect with C.J. – CJPetersonWrites.com